TALES
BY THE TREE

AN ANTHOLOGY OF
HOLIDAY FLASH FICTION

EDITED BY
D.M. KILGORE &
LISA SHAMBROOK

LIVONIA, MICHIGAN

About the Type

This book was set in Adobe Garamond. This font is a digital interpretation of the roman types of Claude Garamond and the italic types of Robert Granjon. Since its release in 1989, Adobe Garamond has become a typographic staple throughout the world of desktop typography and design.

TALES BY THE TREE
Copyright © 2017 BHC Press

All rights reserved. Except as permitted under the U.S. Copyright Act of 1976, no part of this publication may be reproduced, distributed, or transmitted in any form or by any means, or stored in a database or retrieval system, without prior written permission of the publisher.

This book is a work of fiction. The characters, incidents, and dialogue are drawn from the author's imagination and are not to be construed as real. Any resemblance to actual events or persons, living or dead, is entirely coincidental.

Published by BHC Press

Library of Congress Control Number:
2017933753

ISBN: 978-1-946006-70-7

Visit the publisher at:
www.bhcpress.com

Also available in ebook

Table of Contents

11
MARISSA AMES
Grandma's Christmas Sweaters

15
RUTH LONG
Falling

19
LISA SHAMBROOK
Winter Hope

22
JEAN BOOTH
The Long Night Moon

25
RAYMOND HENRI
In the Outside

28
AILSA ABRAHAM
Merry Mythmas

32
MONA BLISS
Day's End

34
LISA V. TOMECEK
A HELL OF A THING

37
LIZZIE KOCH
CHRISTMAS PREPARATIONS

40
JUDY CARPENTER
MERRY AND BRIGHT

44
ERIC MARTELL
NOT AS THEY ARE

48
LESLIE FULTON
HOLLYWOOD NORTH

52
LISA T. CRESSWELL
SPELL SPINNER CHRISTMAS

56
NICK JOHNS
'TWAS THE FIGHT BEFORE CHRISTMAS

59
S.R. BETLER
THE WILD HUNTERS

63
JENNIFER GARRETT
A CHRISTMAS CHANGE

67
BETH AVERY
THE TOWN BENEATH THE LAKE

70
LARA HAYS
THE TALISMAN

74
MARY MACFARLANE
I'LL BE HOME FOR CHRISTMAS

77
ERIC MARTELL
WALLY, THE PENGUIN WHO COULD FLY

81
MARISSA AMES
REBIRTH IN BETHLEHEM

85
SARA DANIELL
SNOWED IN

90
K.R. SMITH
THE LAST SNOWFALL

95
BETH AVERY
JACK FROST STOPS BY FOR A CHAT

97
LAURA JAMEZ
NAUGHTY OR NICE

100
REBECCA FYFE
A CHRISTMAS DANCE

103
MARJIE MYERS
TO THE TOP OF THE TREE

107
TERRY CROUSE
ONE MAGICAL NIGHT

110
REBECKA VIGUS
WHAT IS THIS CHRISTMAS?

114
REBECCA FYFE
THE YULETIDE EXCHANGE

118
TOM MOHAN
SCARRED

121
GLEN DAMIEN CAMPBELL
THE GIFT

125
ERIC SPROLES
CHRISTMAS 1916

127
J.S. BAILEY
SCRATCH

132
RAYMOND HENRI
THE GIVING GIFT

135
MONA BLISS
WHAT'S GOOD FOR THE GOOSE

138
LISA SHAMBROOK
THE LITTLE MOUSE

141
MARISSA AMES
THOMAS'S NEW COAT

145
AILSA ABRAHAM
UNEXPECTED ENCOUNTER

148
ALEX BRIGHTSMITH
PICTURE PERFECT

151
LESLIE FULTON
THE CHRISTMAS LETTER

155
SARAH NICHOLSON
THE ANGEL WHO DIDN'T LIKE CHRISTMAS

159
LISA SHAMBROOK
THE STAR SHONE BRIGHTLY

162
MICHAEL WOMBAT
CLAUSTROPHOBIA

165
LADONNA COLE
ALL THE CHRISTMASSY THINGS

TALES
BY THE TREE

MARISSA AMES
Grandma's Christmas Sweaters

Grandma knitted sweaters every year, from January to November, and gifted them in December. She intertwined yarn into elaborate Christmas trees, stars, and snowy woodland scenes. Grandma's sweaters reminded me of Care Bears spreading Christmas love with bedazzled belly magic.

Every year, I got a sweater from Grandma. Knowing what lay inside, I tore into the box with practiced enthusiasm. I pulled out the mass of festive yarn and held it up to the light of the Christmas tree, gushing about the love and attention she must have taken, just for me.

Then I tucked the sweater back in the box. Twelve boxes sat in my closet, neatly stacked in the far corner behind my old stuffed animals.

"Grandma's visiting for a week," Mom told us. "It would be nice if you wore one of those sweaters while she was here."

I groaned and slumped, but my sister Sarah agreed. Nine-year-olds know nothing about making a stand for fashion.

When Grandma arrived, Sarah waited at the door in a red and green monstrosity. Grandma's hot pink lips stretched taut over her dentures as she pinched Sarah's cheeks.

Sarah grabbed Grandma's wrinkled, spotted hand. "Wanna bake cookies, Gramma?" With that pink smile in place, Grandma waddled into the kitchen after Sarah.

"Where's your sweater?" Mom asked from behind me.

"I'll wear it closer to Christmas," I promised.

The second day, Sarah wore a fuzzy white garment bedazzled with blue rhinestone snowflakes as she held Grandma's yarn. Mom raised her eyebrows as I passed in my t-shirt. I shrugged and moved into the yarn-free zone.

"You're going to disappoint her," Mom accused the next morning.

I shrugged and continued texting.

"Sarah's learning how to knit, and you're ignoring your Grandma. Just wear the sweater, just once."

"I will," I whined, annoyed that I had to look up from my phone.

On the fourth day, I lacerated my foot in Sarah's room. "You left knitting needles on the floor," I said, picking up the bloody awl. "Where did you get these needles?"

"From Gramma," she said, coiling yarn around her wrist. "What should I make with this?"

I shook my head. "You're getting weird," I said, hobbling away to find a Band-Aid.

Mom wouldn't leave me alone. "Wear a sweater," she said, grabbing her hem and stretching it down for emphasis, warping the snowman on the front. "Honestly, what harm could come of wearing one?"

"I don't know," I argued between texts. "I can't risk it."

Mom rolled her eyes. "Come to dinner."

"What are we having?" I asked without looking up from my phone.

"Something soft, with lots of fiber," she said as she shuffled out of my room.

I woke at 4 a.m. to the aroma of chocolate chip cookies. I rubbed my eyes and followed the smell to the kitchen. Decked in boughs of sweater holly, Sarah removed a tray from the oven. On the table, hundreds of cookies cascaded onto the lace runner. She had to have been baking for hours to acquire that many.

I squeaked, "What are you doing? How long have you been baking?"

"Oh, don't bother her," Mom said from behind me. I turned to see her sway past me, wearing slippers and a housecoat, with a red Santa sweater overtop of the coat.

Sarah set the cookie tray on a trivet. "Eat some," she said. "You need some meat on those bones." I flinched back as she tried to pinch my cheek.

On day six, I opened Sarah's underwear drawer to borrow a pair of socks. She wouldn't miss one pair, and I'd have it washed and back in the drawer by tomorrow. The drawer rattled as I pulled it out. My mouth fell open.

Instead of socks, Sarah's drawer was filled with knitting needles of assorted sizes. Hundreds of needles, jammed tightly. I pulled out other drawers to find the same thing: hoarded knitting needles.

"Mom!" I called, wandering about the room.

All of Sarah's clothes sat in a pile in her closet. On her hangers, bags of yarn dangled. A housecoat draped over her headboard. Eight pair of slippers peeked from beneath the bed.

"Mom!" I yelled again, hustling out of the room.

Mom sat in the living room, entwining two long, slender sticks into a network of yarn. Sarah sat on one side of her, and Grandma sat on the other. Reindeer pranced across their chests, ending in a knitted sleigh on Sarah's sweater. On the coffee table sat glasses of Metamucil.

Mom looked up from her knitting. "Do I have to tell you again?" She glared at my designer shirt. "Go put on a sweater!"

I sprinted to my room and yanked my phone out of my pocket.

"911. What is your emergency?"

"Um…" It sounded stupid even before I said it. "My Grandma's Christmas sweaters are turning my family into old-person zombies," I blurted out.

The operator paused. I heard snickering in the background. In a professional and appropriately prudish voice, she said, "Miss, abuse of the 911 system is a crime. If this is not a real emergency, you need to hang up right now, or I will inform the police."

Tears stung my eyes as I watched my thumb hover over the touch screen. The police would not believe me. I lowered my thumb to the "end" icon.

That night I fell asleep with the light on as Mom, Grandma, and Sarah baked fruitcake until dawn.

"Wake up," Sarah called, shaking my shoulder. "It's Christmas!"

I groaned and rubbed my eyes. Exhausted, I had fallen asleep in a chilly room and had woken up cozy and comfortable. I folded my wool-covered arms and sighed.

Mom, Grandma, and Sarah all hovered above me.

"Merry Christmas!" Mom greeted me, pinching my cheek. "What do you want for breakfast?"

I ran my hands over my belly, feeling the texture of miniature plastic lights beneath my palms. Sitting up, I adjusted the green sweater over my chest and said, "Stewed prunes."

RUTH LONG
FALLING

"We were together, I have forgotten the rest."
~ Walt Whitman ~

Her smile is an upside-down parachute as she falls through the dusky twilit sky, drifting past bare branches, frosted windows, and colored lights.

The wind catches her up and sweeps her across the snow-slick street, through bow-bedecked cedar wreaths, and over the tops of brightly colored hats.

As she swirls above the park, a brass band strikes up a holiday tune and a crowd gathers around the makeshift platform. While the song's final refrain hangs in the crisp December air, a city official unveils the new bronze statue overlooking the ice rink.

When a collective cheer rises from the crowd and the sculptor's mouth curves with creative satisfaction, she descends, sliding across his lower lip, drawing out the moment, absorbing every sensation in hopes of imprinting it on her memory—the soft warmth of his lip, the rough exhale of his breath, the sweet caress of his tongue.

And then it is over, and she is melting, dripping off his mouth and plummeting to the ground. It doesn't hurt, and she isn't scared. She's done it—melting, not kissing—thousands of times in her life. Falling, freezing, melting, and evaporating. She'll do it again tomorrow and every day that follows.

But as she splashes into the cold, damp ground, a spark shoots through her and something flickers to life. Her vision skews and she stumbles. But how can that be? She doesn't have legs.

A hand catches her elbow and a masculine voice says, "My apologies, ma'am. I—oh! It's you!"

His voice is like a melody, like wind through cedars or a brook over pebbles, and her ears drink it in.

She should reply but how? Mouths are a mystery to her. If she opens her lips, will the words in her head rush out like a river?

Still holding her by the arm, he says "Here, take my coat. You must be freezing in that lightweight sweater."

His warmth and scent envelop her as he wraps her in the heavy wool, and his gray eyes are piercing as they evaluate her, as if comparing her—but to what?

She looks away, unsure of herself, of what is happening, of how long it will last.

He lifts a gloved hand toward the statue and says, "I'm sorry if I'm making you uncomfortable. It's just that you look so much like her."

She glances at the beautiful bronze figure and touches her own face, wondering if it's true.

It's only one word, but she manages to make it audible. "Skate."

His elegant face dissolves into a boyish grin and taking her hand, he heads to the skate rental booth.

The gentleman behind the counter smiles and says, "What size, Miss? Seven, right?"

She nods only because she has no answer and as the sculptor crouches to lace her feet into the skates, it appears seven is indeed correct. After lacing his own skates, he rises, tucks her hand in the crook of his arm, and leads her onto the ice. He puts an arm around her waist and they slide off across the rink.

Steadied by his bulk and proximity, she allows herself to experience the rushing of wind in her hair, the sting of crisp winter air against her cheeks, and the sweet tang of apple cider in her nose.

A tangle of thoughts and feelings bubble up and spill out her mouth in a burst of laughter, and there's an emotion lodged in her chest, something warm and heavy and unfamiliar.

When the sun begins its descent, he leans close and says, "Are you ready for cider or hot chocolate?"

She smiles and manages a second word. "Lovely."

He seats her in the shelter of the gazebo and goes to get their drinks.

When she is alone, a pale visage appears to her. "Mr. Frost sent me to advise you that you must relinquish your magic by midnight if you wish to retain this body."

Until now, she'd floated through life, a lacy little snowflake, her life dependent on magic and the camaraderie of fellow elements.

She'd cashed in every credit to make her wish for a holiday kiss from the sculptor come true, but Jack had taken it upon himself to change the outcome and turned her into a human. Now he was offering her permanent status as a mortal. Should she accept it?

But before she can respond, the messenger disappears as the sculptor returns.

He sets the warm cups on the railing and sits beside her. "My behavior today has been—uncharacteristic. It's just that I feel as though the face I dreamed of and created, that knowing smile, those laughing eyes, have come to life in you. Forgive me. I haven't even asked your name."

"Crystal," she says, pleased to know this answer.

He takes her hand again, as he has all afternoon, as if he covets her attention and touch, as if such familiarity is natural. "Seeing as I appear incapable of banishing this schoolboy behavior in your company, I'm impulsively inviting you to attend the museum gala this evening as my guest. Please say yes, Crystal!"

She looks at him and the heaviness in her chest becomes something with claws, as though she can't breathe, can't get air.

She reaches for his face, for his strong jaw, for his beautiful mouth, the thing that brought her here, to this man, to this moment.

Kissing him is like falling, like whirling through secret galaxies, like dancing in the thumbprints of the gods. Surely this magic, mouths praying one to another, exceeds her elemental power and is worth the price of her immortality.

"Stay," she says against his lips. "I'll stay, Ezra."

He kisses her nose. "You know my name?"

She nods, but how can she explain it? She's been falling for him all her life, in a thousand rains and sleets, in rivers and oceans, in snowstorms and frosty windows.

LISA SHAMBROOK
Winter Hope

Gossamer threads hung, decorated with frozen diamonds, and beneath the lacy webs Winter rested her head on the stony floor. Swirls of vapor rose from her nostrils and tiny blue flames licked across her tongue. She sighed.

An amber glow suffused the sky with light, banishing the indigo skyline over the horizon, and the vista smoldered beneath an ethereal haze. Snow clothed the valleys, and ice clung to every rock and ridge. Icing-sugared trees blended the woods together, evergreens bathed in a blanket of white and leafless trees stood dipped in sherbet. A cotton-wool carpet covered the grass before the cave and red berries shone like rubies peeping through earth's crystal mantle. Lakes shone like glass, and early rising village folk danced across the sheets of ice.

Winter yawned and those below who glanced up at the ridge watched billowing mist spiral down the precipice, collecting in pockets of cloud across the valley. Those early morning folk pulled their woolly hats down over their pink-tipped ears and shivered.

As dawn spread her fingers of light across the horizon, Winter smiled to herself. She recalled her preceding season's hibernation, and the delight of the valley people as she'd arrived one late November day, bringing swathes of white and an energizing, but bitter, wind. They'd hurried out of their houses, clothed in colors so bright, and the wondrous noise of joy had risen high into the echoing mountains. As she'd twirled and soared, she'd conjured blizzards, and flurries, and danced all day long. That night she'd flown across the inky sky, frosting the skeletal forests and sifting snow atop everything in sight.

Now the dragon kept watch and waited.

As the sun rose, she basked in its warmth then she stood and stretched. Her scales clattered as she shook herself and glitter showered the mountain, the breeze catching and swirling it across the hills and vales. Impatience flicked her tail, and she shook out her wings. Huge wings, overlaid with intricate and elaborate frosted filigree, fanned and fluttered. Winter lifted her head, gazed across the land, and memories of solstice, the recent longest night, made her heart leap and a deep pink blush rippled across her body. Her smile grew and anticipation tingled. Just one more night, and he'd be home.

She waited.

Dusk fell and the sky turned as red as the holly berries before dipping behind the mountain range. Winter could barely contain her excitement, and she launched away from the cliff, floating across the sapphire sky. The dragon blew gently, clearing the clouds, leaving the sky full only of glittering stars. She glided silently past each house; her own smoke mingling with the spiraling plumes from chimneys everywhere. She watched children hang stockings on their bedposts or on the mantelpiece. She smiled at last minute gift wrapping and inhaled the delicious fragrance of wood smoke, mulled wine and cinnamon. She drifted across the night breathing out fresh flurries of snow, and painting windows with the most delicate lattice curls of ice.

Stars glimmered as she retired back to her cave, and just once she thought she heard bells tinkling, but maybe it was the frost on her scales.

~ TALES BY THE TREE ~

It was early, not even dawn had stirred, when bells did indeed chime and Winter woke. She snorted, and her scales quivered as she moved swiftly from her bed of oak leaves to the mouth of her grotto. There on the snowy ridge, stood several reindeer, antlers draped with moss and holly, and Winter's heart leaped.

The dragon danced in the snow, and the reindeer eyed her warily. More reindeer wandered, moving off into the forest, and from the woods came a deep chuckle. Winter moved forward, her heart pounding within her chest and a man stepped out of the trees.

Father Winter stood before her in one of his many guises, and she spread her wings whipping up a blizzard. The tempest flew about the stout man, snowflakes settled on his face and in his beard, coating his figure and turning him momentarily into a snowman.

Spirals of star-studded smoke wreathed the snow-laden figure, and his reindeer took off into the sky. Smoke and fire fizzed and crackled, and Winter's own ice blue flames sparked amid her roiling, swirling snowflakes. The smoky column intensified and coiled up into the sky, and then in an explosion of snow and ice and fireworks, a crimson dragon burst forth from the smoke.

His scales gleamed, and his wings shuddered as he stepped forward and extended his flared nostrils to Winter, his mate.

Now free from Yuletide obligation, Father Winter returned to his favorite form. His eyes roamed across Winter, his breath caught and smoke eddied as he exhaled. As dawn whispered and church bells rang down in the valley, two dragons with wings the colors of mistletoe and holly berries, rose into the sky and the season of goodwill began.

JEAN BOOTH

The Long Night Moon

"Grandmother, will you tell us a story?"

"Oh, child! I am old and don't remember many stories," the old woman replied with a glint in her eyes. "What would you like to hear?"

"Tell of how the sun loved the moon so much that he died every day so she could live," the child said eagerly.

"Ah, that one," she said with a sigh.

Carefully she settled herself deeper into the pillows, her grandchildren crowding around to hear her story.

LONG AGO, before the land grew life, there was the sun.

He was called Arona.

Arona was strong, powerful, full of life and energy. He proudly lit the skies, illuminating the darkest corners, keeping the night at bay.

The people of the land loved Arona, and he loved them. They smiled and thanked him as they went about their lives.

Arona watched as they fell in love.

Soon the people who so loved Arona were too distracted to talk with him or even grant him a small smile. And Arona found himself growing lonely.

It was midsummer's eve when she appeared, a small, silver orb in the sky.

Arona was intrigued by her appearance.

He inched his way closer to her until the day they finally met.

"What a lovely silver color you possess," he said to her in greeting, shining as brightly as he could.

"I came from night to see your bright light," she replied. "You shine so brightly all the time, certainly you need to rest?"

Arona was taken aback at her request. A sun as strong as he had no need for sleep!

"You are mistaken," he explained, shining brighter still. "I will shine and protect the land until I can no longer burn."

He thought he saw her shrug.

"Then I will stay and keep you company. I am Luna."

With nothing to do to occupy her time, Luna danced across the sky. She would twirl around and disappear into the night, where Arona couldn't follow. It was a forbidden place, and he would die if he went.

Many months went by in this manner. They would pass each other, say hello.

Arona grew curious of Luna's trips in the dark.

"What do you do when you leave?" he asked one day.

"I smile down on those below and shine for them," was her reply.

"How is it that you shine?" he demanded.

"I reflect the love I have for you and remind the night of your majestic glow."

He dimmed with speechlessness.

They hung together in the sky, one bright, one light and danced until he realized that he too, loved Luna.

"I must go, I've been gone too long," she whispered with regret.

Leaving Arona, she went into the night.

He followed, risking death to glimpse her light.

What he saw caused a tear to fall.

She shone with a beautiful silver glow, one that was too light to shine with his bright aura.

When she returned, they danced together until they reached the expanse of night.

"I grow weary and must leave to shine my light," she admitted softly with regret.

"You love this land, as I. I have seen you shine and know that you must glow to have life. Let me show you how I love you," Arona said, kissing her softly before entering the night to die.

Luna's light grew bright and brighter still, until she glowed with her soft, silvery light. She wept for Arona, her tears opening holes in the night sky, reflecting their love with soft light. She could not hear the soft hush of joy that passed through the land, she just wished for her friend.

Hours went by, too long to count, and Luna met the other side of the land. Out of the darkness that hid the night, pale fingers reached. They stretched across the sky until at last; Arona pulled himself free from his deathly trip into the dark.

And from that first Winter Solstice, Arona and Luna shared the sky. Arona dies to give Luna life and she shines bright with her love for him. You can still see them dance, embracing one another as they cross paths in the sky if you so chose.

GRANDMOTHER FINISHED the story as the children slept around her.

She looked up into the night sky, toward the brilliant silver light of Luna's full, long night moon and smiled.

RAYMOND HENRI
IN THE OUTSIDE

Holrune had settled into a soft blue chair with unforgiving wooden arms. Aging, yet timeless, decorations festooned the triage waiting room with a garish mix of holiday traditions, offering Holrune more invisibility than he could have hoped for. Detection was the enemy in this kind of work. Yes, this time of year made work much, much easier for a healer-observer. Anyone looking his way would only see a silver three-foot plastic tree wired with little blue lights. No one would look close enough to see that his brown skin was actually comprised of scales melded with blending clay and, as long as he didn't open his mouth fully, it would appear much smaller, and by extension, human.

It had been quite some time since someone new had come into the hospital. Everyone here had been checked, cleared, and rechecked just to be sure no trace of interspecies disease remained. Holrune started the book he was reading over again and eavesdropped on those nearby to avoid getting too caught up in his own thoughts. Human conversation, the need for vocalization for that matter, amused him. So much energy and consumption of time dedicated to endless strings of words enervated by streams of emotions when often the speaker was only really trying to say "I care about you" or "I care about me." It seemed humans had such a hard time dealing with root truths that they constructed entire languages to avoid them.

"Every year I find myself wrestling with how I reconcile Christmas," one man was saying to his female companion, both of them half a room away with their backs to Holrune. "Being atheist, I'm constantly at odds with the whole existence of the holiday, its origins, and all that. But, I have these rigid traditions with my family. I mean, how do I participate in a celebration of something I spend so much time disavowing?"

"So, it...what?" the female companion responded. "Uh, makes you feel like a hypocrite?"

"Yeah. I guess that's the problem. I guess I'm starting to feel like celebrating at all is hypocritical."

"Well, look at it this way. You're taking this time to celebrate the better qualities of humanity. Generosity. Kindness. Love. All the beautiful aspects of our species. And you're also saying that you don't need to be part of a religion to recognize and celebrate those things."

"Hmm. I think I see what you're saying."

The better qualities of humanity? Holrune figured there were probably just enough of those to spend one time of the year to celebrate. That's about it, though. Still, the conversation left him dwelling on the matter more personally. He almost wished there was some sort of equal celebration back home, but Christ wasn't born to his world. Didn't die to save it either. As far as Holrune knew, his planet didn't even have original sin. If it did, no one was talking about it, and it's the kind of thing to talk about.

It started to bother Holrune more the longer the night went. An atheist could choose to participate in a religious tradition whilst being antagonistic to that religion, and yet Holrune, whether he believed or not, didn't even feel the invitation. He wanted it. Pangs of jealousy pulsed through him with desire for fellowship, cheer, surprise, wonder, and appreciation. His existence of hiding in shadows and diagnosing and treating humans with alien diseases now felt more solitary and pitiful than anything he had witnessed in human life. Perhaps it made humans superior to be able to connect on a more personal and verbal level, despite the pitfalls of their inherit limitations. That thought had certainly never crossed Holrune's mind before.

Suddenly and silently, Luthon sat on the other side of the waiting room tree. Holrune's shift was coming to an end. Luthon appeared more like an old man than Holrune on a bad day. It was apparent Luthon needed to spend more time on blending his clay. If he wasn't careful, he'd not only attract attention, he'd be admitted.

"Been running away from your footsteps, Holrune?" Luthon asked telepathically.

"No. It's been quiet. There were a few glandinoids and jumpers but mostly waxons complex. Not even much of that. Easy night," Holrune reported.

"Didn't see any shartitis?"

"It's been over a week since I have. We must have gotten ahead of that one."

"I hope so. Well, you go and get some rest. I left some treats for you on the table in your room. Merry Christmas, friend."

Holrune was momentarily unsettled. "Thank you, Luthon. Merry Christmas." A welcome spread of warmth radiated from his belly. "That makes me happy."

"I care about you," Luthon said, busying himself with a book as he officially took over duties.

AILSA ABRAHAM
MERRY MYTHMAS

K eira'd had an overdose of Christmas and not in a good way. Sister Mary-Kathleen and the staff at the home had done their best. That was the problem, they were trying too hard. All the jollies were forced and unnatural. The other kids were at church, and she'd only escaped through complaining of a bellyache. Said it was that crap dinner they served up last night. She hated eating turkey, threw the sprouts at Ashok and deliberately slopped the sludgy gravy all over the table.

Yeah, but why should this year be any different? Christmas at home (snort) had always been Mum and "whoever she was with" getting off their faces and shouting, then taking it out on her. Even that time in the foster family it'd been a nightmare with their son telling her that she wasn't wanted, that she was a tramp, while being sweetness and light in front of his parents.

There'd only be Mrs. Dillon downstairs, and she was deaf as a post, so she'd have the TV on ear-blasting level. Now was the only time to do it if she was going, but she'd have to be quick. Nipping into the kitchen, she filched a few notes from Mrs. Dillon's handbag and in ten minutes she'd legged it across the fields and was thumbing a lift on the main London road. There wasn't much traffic, but an older woman in a smart car pulled over and gave her a lift.

Keira'd dreamed up a story. She was hitching to the station to get a train to meet her brother in London. She'd be spending New Year's with him and his mates. Kiera was very inventive. Unfortunately, the woman was a nosy old cow and started asking a lot of questions. Seeing a burger van in a lay-by coming up, Keira said that she was feeling carsick and needed to stop. The woman looked worried and annoyed, but said she couldn't hang around.

Result!

The only customer there was a cool-looking goth female with a spiky punk hairdo dyed jet black with a shiny purple reflection. Keira ordered a burger and a mug of tea, but when she felt in her jeans pocket, the money she'd nicked from the handbag was gone. The guy behind the counter snapped his fingers.

"Come on, kid. If you order stuff you gotta pay for it, that's £2.50"

"S'okay, Tony. Put it on my tab." The goth exhaled a stream of lilac smoke from her black-painted lips and thrust out a black, fingerless-gloved hand, the nails matching the lipstick.

"Tink."

"Keira" She shook hands awkwardly. Her new benefactress pointed at the beat-up plastic table and chairs.

"Might as well take the weight off." She had a pint-sized mug of black coffee and chain smoked weird cigarettes that seemed to give off slight sparks as she inhaled. "Pissed off with Christmas, then?"

"How d'ye guess?"

"Well, kid out here on her own this early on Boxing Day isn't having a good time. Right?"

"I'm going to…"

"Yeah, whatever." The goth waved a dismissive hand as if to say *I know you're going to tell me a pack of lies, and I'm not interested.*

Keira felt ashamed. It wasn't a familiar feeling for her but this weirdo had just paid for her burger so she said, "Yeah, I hate Christmas."

"True. What's to like?"

"I mean—that nativity stuff. Like, born in a stable? Right!"

"Yeah. Expect those two might believe it though." Tink pointed at a derelict parked car. A young man sat chewing his nails in the driver's seat while the woman lay asleep in the back with a tiny baby on her chest wrapped in an anorak. "She had the baby in there last night."

"But why don't they go to a hospital?" Keira was aghast.

"Illegals. Scared to death they'll get deported. Way it is."

Defensively, Keira nodded but said, "Okay, but all that stuff about animals speaking at Christmas and that?"

"Don't believe a word of it!" a passing Labrador remarked as he lifted his leg against the back of the caravan.

"Oi! Watch where you're doing that, mate!" the plastic snowman on the caravan door grumbled.

"Sorry, pal. I expect you're another of those Christmas myths she don't believe in."

Things were turning decidedly weird, and Keira wondered if Tink's odd smokes were the reason.

"I suppose you're going to magic up Santa now to make me think he exists."

"Magic up? What, like now I'm some kind of fairy or something?" The goth gave her a twisted smile and shook her head 'til all her jewelry rattled. "Gimme a break, kid. You don't believe in fairies."

The dog, the snowman, and Tony the burger-seller all suppressed giggles until Tink shot them a look. Leaning forward on the table she glared into Keira's eyes.

"Do you believe in happy endings then?"

"Not for people like me."

"Okay. What would you like for Christmas, Keira? Say I'm the Secret Millionaire."

"A family." It was out before Keira could stop it. Tears filled her eyes.

Tink produced a newspaper from her studded shoulder bag. "Recognize anyone?"

The paper was several years old but next to a photo was the headline *Hunt Continues for Missing Millie*.

Tink retrieved two helmets from Tony and grabbed the stunned Keira's arm.

"Come on, kid. Guess I'm going to make several people's Christmases this year. Get on the bike and hold on."

As the Happy Endings Fairy and Keira roared off up the road, they didn't hear the Labrador say to Tony, "Pity, I was getting quite used to this. All back to Santa's for a quick pint, then?"

"It's on you," said the snowman. "You peed on my feet!"

MONA BLISS
Day's End

He gently lowered his bulky, aging body into the beach chair and put his ice cold beer into the chair's cupholder. His soft white feet stretched out before him, clad in tourist store flip-flops. The sun felt like warm honey all over his body as slowly the night's work eased out of him. For the last few years this was where he finished up, Australia, on the beach with a beer.

The first year he did it he only stayed for an hour or so, just long enough to drink a beer at the beachside bar. The next year he just couldn't resist taking his boots off and getting his tired old feet into the warm, scratchy sand. The year after that he bought a whole set of beach clothes, got a chair and some sunglasses, and spent hours baking the exhaustion and cold out of his bones. That was the year he made friends with Ruby the bartender. She was the only one who knew who he really was. She kept his beach stuff for him so he could change when he arrived.

But even in his disguise, people had a hard time leaving him alone. He glanced to his left and saw a lovely young woman sunbathing on a towel. She looked over at him and smiled. He nodded pleasantly and then leaned back in his chair and closed his eyes.

"Excuse me, I'm sorry to bother you, but you look just like Santa Claus. You wouldn't happen to be him, would you?" she asked with a mischievous little smile.

He turned his head in her direction, lifted his sunglasses and squinted at her saying, "Why yes, Ginny, I am. And unless you want to end up on the Naughty List for the next ten years, I suggest you stop lying to your mother about Sunday dinners, stop sneaking off at lunch for quickies with your boss and stop stealing office supplies every time you get mad at him for being married." Then he closed his eye and started to softly snore.

The startled young woman jumped up, grabbed her stuff and ran off the each. Suddenly the old man felt a shadow over him and opened his eyes in irritation only to face Ruby from the bar. She looked irritated.

"What?" he said defensively.

"You did it again, didn't you?" she said as she sat down in the sand next to him handing him his basket of fries.

"Well, they shouldn't ask if they don't want to know."

"Ya know, Kris, nobody really wants Santa Claus to call them on their shit. They like you better as an idea than a reality, and I have to deal with the fall out everytime you do that little trick. So, knock it off or your wife is going to hear about your little 'delay' getting home and your ass will be ice cold North Pole toast. You get me?"

Kris ignored her as he slowly chewed the delicious fried potatoes, licking salt and grease from his fingers. Ruby shook her head, laughing and said, "Wave when you're ready for another beer." She got up and walked back up the beach.

LISA V. TOMECEK
A Hell of a Thing

"Come in from the cold, Uncle."

I look up from the window to see him standing there by the open door: tall and lean and maybe thirty, with an easy smile, stubble, shaggy hair. And flip-flops.

Who wears flip-flops in the snow?

He's always been like that, my nephew. I suspect I'll never understand why.

"You look like hell, Uncle," he says, and means it. I take in the jumble of thrift store denim and flannel and chuckle at the irony.

"I'm fine," I say. I shrug deeper into my overcoat—black, wool, made in Italy—and heft my coffee. The steam spirals up in the chill. "Just out for a walk."

"Don't lie, Uncle. You didn't walk."

He frowns and waves a hand at the car that sits idling at the curb. The engine rumbles like a drowsing beast; the parking lights pulse red, wash the icy slush on the streets with blood.

"Come in. Bring your driver, too. We're sitting down to dinner. Everyone's there—well, except you."

I know already. I've seen them gathered around the table, watched a long time. The memories of younger days wash over me, and for a moment, I think about it. But—

"No. I'm fine. I have things to do. Business meetings. Paperwork. Hostile takeovers. You know how it goes."

But I know he doesn't; he's never been the corporate type. Still, he lets me play the game, and he smiles that easy smile again.

"It's been a long time—too long. Everyone would be glad to see you."

There he's wrong. There I know better. I shrug and swallow my coffee. It's bitter.

"Your dad and I don't get along. We haven't. We won't."

"You could," he says, "if you tried."

"I don't think so," I tell him. "Sometimes things go too far for making up."

He frowns again. The falling snow clings to his shirt, lights in his hair. "You know I don't agree."

"And you know I think you're too idealistic for your own good."

A sudden sadness comes over him. He lifts up his hands, plaintive. "I wish you'd stop this, Uncle. Every year, you show up on the doorstep, and every year you refuse to come in. Just—why?"

I smile. It's thin, wistful. I taste the spoiled memories. They're bitter, like the coffee.

"Pride, kid. Pride's a hell of a thing."

I turn back to the waiting car.

"Should I tell him you came, Uncle?" he calls after.

I don't bother to turn back.

"No."

There's a long pause, then—

"Merry Christmas, Uncle," he says quietly, in that way without malice that I'll never understand.

35

The car door opens. The heat welling from within washes the chill off my bones. I sit down, settle in, shut the door. My driver leans in from the front seat. His eyes catch the streetlights and glow, molten pools of red. They weren't always that way.

Neither were mine.

"Where to, Boss?"

"Away," I tell him. "Anywhere but here."

LIZZIE KOCH
Christmas Preparations

Evie and Leah had done a great job in foraging for holly and fir cones under the watchful eye of Ben. The pile sat on the table. Lisa heard her girls laughing as they cleaned up. Her girls' laughter was infectious but a rarity these days. Looking at the table, Lisa thought back to the days when she was little and decorated fir cones in glitter for a table centerpiece, using the holly to place carefully around thick cream candles. Sometimes she would decorate the candles with images of Father Christmas or angels. Angels were her favorite and at times, Lisa felt she had her own personal angel looking over her. She had to. After what she and her family had been through, had survived, here they were, ready to celebrate Christmas…if Lucas came home. There was always an "if" now.

Lisa wandered over to the boundary of their farm, the winter sun bright but weak in heat as it was every winter. But she was thankful for it as it brightened up an otherwise gray world. A light, cooling breeze rolled over her and brought with it the saltiness of the sea just a mile away. Straining her ears, she thought she heard the freedom of the waves crashing against the stony beach.

"Mum, do we have any glitter?"

"I don't know, Evie, you'll have to look." They'd only been at the farm for a month and trying to make it secure was priority rather than searching for arts and crafts. So far, the farmhouse was proving the sanctuary they needed; a greenhouse with seasonal fruits and vegetables, a thriving vegetable garden, two pigs which from the previous owners were pets going by the name plates on the pen: Salt and Pepper. Once the boundary was secure, the farm made the ideal home. With vehicles in good working order, they made runs to the nearby town and beyond.

"I'm sure the boys are fine," Kelly said, joining Lisa at the fence. "They know exactly what they're doing. I've turned the oven on all ready." Lisa loved Kelly's optimism; better to have even a pinch of it in this new world rather than the bucket load of pessimism Lisa carried.

"Mum, look what I found," Evie shouted, running from the house, carrying a plastic box. "It's full of paints, glitter, sequins and look." She held up a homemade angel made from a toilet roll, lace and an overload of cotton wool. "Can we put it on top of the tree?"

"Sure." She wiped a tear. "Argh, this is so stupid! But I used to have a box like that. And now we're using someone else's memories, living in someone else's home. It feels wrong."

"The home was empty, like it was waiting for us. We need a home and to lead a normal life. It's important for the kids. That's all that matters."

The sound of an engine and tires on gravel made them both rigid; never knowing who was driving down toward the farm until the familiar blue truck came into view.

"Did you get the turkey?" Kelly asked as Lucas and Sam stepped from the truck.

"Not quite. But got us a chicken or two. They're flapping in the sack," Sam said with a chuckle.

"You mean they're alive? I can't deal with that," Lisa moaned.

~ TALES BY THE TREE ~

"You're gonna have to deal with a lot worse; there's a group heading this way, and I don't mean chickens," Lucas said, grabbing his hold all. "Get everyone ready." He never used the Z word with Lisa. Even though they were in the midst of a zombie infestation, the Z word sent her into a blind panic and that wasn't good to anyone despite facing zombie combat on many occasions.

"Couldn't you pick them off before you got here?" Lisa said, panicking.

"Too many. We'll be fine here." The group gathered as Lucas handed out weapons. With glitter-covered hands, Evie grabbed her crude looking spear with ease and stood at her post as did Leah and Kelly's teenage son, Ben. "Now remember, the head, you must aim for the head, twice to make sure. We've all got each other's backs so the sooner we do this, the sooner Christmas starts. You good Lisa?" Lucas saw the determination in Lisa's eyes but her shaking arm was evident. "I can see them. About twenty of them." Lucas rushed back to the truck and surprised everyone as Christmas music blared out.

It didn't matter what the circumstances, a blast of Slade wishing it was Christmas every day, lifted everyone's spirit as zombies snarled and gnashed at the fence, clawing only air before dropping with a head split like a melon.

Silent Night drifted across the farm as the last zombie fell, piled high against the fence. Lucas walked over to Evie and Leah, both bloody but unharmed. Holding their hands, Lucas squeezed tight. "Good job girls," he whispered, looking over to Lisa. "Seeing as you've just dispatched half a dozen zombies, I think you can handle the chickens," he said grinning at her. "Come on girls, let's start Christmas.

JUDY CARPENTER
Merry and Bright

D'Vee entered the large room and said a general "hello" to her friends. It was Saturday morning, Christmas Eve, and she was in a merry mood. All her friends responded in kind.

"Well, don't you all look festive?" Her friends lounged on fleece blankets printed with ornaments, stockings, and other Christmas symbols. She shook her head, making the bells on her felt antlers peal, and the room erupted in happy response.

She poured tea from her thermos into a travel mug and took a long draft. Sighing in contentment, she replaced the lid and set the thermos on the table by the door.

As she worked the room, she greeted each friend by name and exchanged kisses with them. Suddenly her gaze was drawn to a pair of dark, dark brown eyes at the other end of the room. *Someone new.*

The owner of the eyes stood, and D'Vee pulled in a quick breath. He was magnificent! Dark brown hair with streaks of silver, an expressive face… She moved toward him, taking her time, trying not to appear too eager.

She made it to his side, but hoping to present a professional persona, she took his chart and read.

"Hmm," she said out loud and looked at him out of the corner of her eyes. "Corky. There appears to be nothing wrong with you, Corky. So why are you here? Not that I'm complaining."

"Yip!" was the reply.

D'Vee set her mug on top of the kennel, bent down and opened the door. The little Yorkie jumped into her arms and lavished her face with wet, sloppy kisses.

"Aww, I think you like me!" D'Vee said with a giggle.

"Ahem." The voice behind her took D'Vee by surprise. She turned around quickly and looked up into chocolate brown eyes with long curly lashes.

"You're blond," she said. "You're not supposed to have brown eyes."

The chocolate brown eyes blinked. "I'll…tell my mother."

"Oh. I guess that sounded rather rude."

"Rather." But the mouth below the nose below the chocolate brown eyes twitched. "Why are you fondling my dog?" he asked.

"Corky the Yorkie is yours?" D'Vee tried to choke it back but the giggle bubbled out. "Please tell me you inherited this dog. And its name."

"What? I don't look like the type to give a Yorkie a quirky name like Corky?"

D'Vee laughed as she wiggled her eyebrows. "He's a little porky."

Chocolate Brown Eyes sighed. "Yeah, I've been a little bad in giving him table scraps. But we've both been on a diet, and he's actually lost a pound.

"I'm Alex Lurkey, the new vet." He extended his hand.

Again, D'Vee giggled as she took his hand in hers. "Any relation to Turkey?"

"What? Oh, I see. Turkey Lurkey. Henny Penny. The sky is falling… No. No relation. And you are…?"

"D'Vee Devoh. I volunteer on weekends."

"You're kidding, right? You are Devo, D-E-V-O?"

"Yeah, I get that a lot. But it's really Devoh, D-E-V-O-H."

"Your name is D'Vee Devoh, and you're making fun of Corky the Yorkie and Alex Lurkey?"

D'Vee eyed him for a long moment and then replied, "I guess I have my nerve, huh?"

"Mm-hmm." Alex nodded.

D'Vee found herself mesmerized by the chocolate brown eyes but finally shook herself free. "Well, anyway, I'm glad, though sad, Corky the Yorkie is spoken for. I already have three cats and two ferrets. Though I've always been a sucker for a fine pair of brown eyes, and as the saying goes, there's always room for one more."

Suddenly Alex's head dropped back slightly, and his eyes narrowed as his nostrils flared. "What's that wonderful smell?"

"What? The Lysol?"

"No, nothing medicinal. It's—spicy."

"Oh. You must mean my chai."

"Shy?"

"No, I'm pretty much of an extrovert." D'Vee bit her lower lip, trying to suppress another giggle. Alex gave her a mock glare and she added, "Chai. Spicy Asian tea. Would you like some?"

"I don't know. It smells wonderful, but I think I had it once at Starbucks and didn't like it."

"Starbucks? Pish tosh." D'Vee curled her nose. "Their chai is as good and authentic as Kroger's frozen pizza is good and authentic." She put Corky back in his kennel. She drank the rest of the chai in her mug then took it to the sink by the door. She rinsed it out and retrieved the thermos, filled the mug, and handed it to Alex.

He took the mug and, after sniffing it, took a drink. "Mmm," he said. "Mmm."

D'Vee giggled again as he turned up the mug and took a long drink and repeated, "Mmm."

"I take it you like it," D'Vee said.

He wiped chai from his upper lip with a knuckle. "It's wonderful. Better than coffee. Almost."

D'Vee didn't giggle this time. She laughed, and Alex looked at her strangely. "What?" she asked.

"Do that again," he said.

"Do what?"

"Laugh. It sounded like…Christmas. You know. Merry and… bright." His voice trailed off, and a light pink stain washed over his cheeks.

D'Vee looked at him, her mouth open, and finally managed to clear her throat. "No one has ever said anything nicer to me." She smiled.

"You don't have any husbands or boyfriends hanging around, do you?"

"No, as a matter of fact. How about you? Any wives or girlfriends?"

"No, as a matter of fact. Do you want to get some lunch later?"

"Yeah. Yeah, I would." D'Vee grinned, and Alex grinned back. "Would you like some more chai?"

"Oh, yeah."

A little bit later D'Vee and Alex munched on Big Macs and fries. That evening they made chai and watched *White Christmas* on TV. By New Year's Day Corky, the cats, and the ferrets were all friends.

Upon reflection, D'Vee and Alex decided there was definitely something magical about the Christmas season.

ERIC MARTELL
Not as They Are

Six glasses of water, four trips to the bathroom, five hundred and eleven giggles. Finally, three small people were asleep in what used to be my bed, and I was free to go about my nightly rounds. My wife was trapped under an assortment of limbs, but I'd taken the opportunity during one of the assaults to lie down on the floor. To free myself, I only had to pry a tiny fist off my index finger. Stifling a groan at my stiff back, I mouthed "thank you" to my wife and got a sleepy smile in return.

I could still smell the wood smoke in the air as I made my way down the stairs to the living room. The glow of the fire reminded me of Christmases from long ago when my belief in the mystical was stronger and more innocent, and I could still imagine a world where there would always be someone to take care of me. The kids hadn't yet grown into the jaded cynicism I knew would dominate their teenage years, but I had to fight against the desire to show them what was really out the door, if only they would just look. I didn't believe in some treacly Hallmark Channel version of childhood, but there was strength in seeing the world not as it was, but as you imagined it could be, and I wasn't ready to take that away from them.

My wife had gotten most of the gifts wrapped while I had the kids out shopping for something special for her, and they were stacked neatly in the basement closet. That was the kind of magic I'd come to appreciate more as I'd gotten older. The magic of dependability, of someone showing you they cared about you in myriad small ways that other people wouldn't even notice. Expecting more than that was a good path to the shrink's office or the bottom of a bottle.

The glow of the lights through the pine needles threw shadows around the room, and I let my eyes grow unfocused as I placed the last gift around the tree. We'd had a good year, and I knew the kids would be excited as hours of careful wrapping turned into fodder for a landfill in minutes. Snatching a cookie from the coffee table, I sat back on the couch and stared at nothing—just shapes and colors and shadows, losing myself in the act of chewing.

Every year, we read *'Twas the Night Before Christmas* to the kids, passing down the legacy of mythmaking to another generation. It wasn't the night before anything anymore, except the night before the 5 a.m. after-Christmas sales, but whoever wrote an ode to that wouldn't include luxurious language like "more rapid than eagles, his coursers they came"—a modern-day writer would say "his reindeer were fast." We'd lost a lot more than the innocent belief in Santa Claus—we'd lost a belief in a beauty beyond the efficient buck.

The wind howled outside, and I turned to watch snow start to fall. They'd said it was too warm this year for a white Christmas, but their models are complex and imperfect. Guess the kids would get a chance to break out the new winter boots we'd bought them after all. The snow was awfully bright tonight, a pure white that glowed in the moonlight.

But there was a new moon tonight. I'd made a comment about it during the whole "moon on the breast of the new-fallen snow" line during reading time tonight, and I'd even doublechecked it on my phone. As I tried to wrap my brain around what I was seeing, the snow got even brighter, forcing me to lift an arm to shade my eyes. And then came the flash. And the voice.

It is your turn, Charlie.

There was no one around to speak to me, nor to speak to, but that voice was too intense to disregard. Impossible or not, it was there. "Uh, my turn for what?"

To believe.

"I do—I did. There's no point anymore. The kids do. That's enough."

Belief lies with the giver. You must give to believe.

"Give? I give all the time. At work. Here. Look at that pile of gifts! And the Salvation Army—well, not them anymore. But Toys for Tots. Gifts for soldiers. The wishing well at the mall."

Not things. Not money. To the empty heart, money is cold comfort.

"Then what?"

To see the world not as it is, but as it could be.

"But how—how do I give that? People see what they want to."

No. People see what they've been taught to.

"So—my kids? Change what I teach them? Am I doing it wrong?"

Yes. But no. This is not for them. Your children are your daily burden and gift. This is for the other. The life you cannot touch, but who needs it.

"Why—why me? What's special about me?"

It is your turn. Be not afraid. The giving is not without rewards for the giver. Open your mind to the possibilities.

I didn't respond this time, but did what the voice said. I thought about what I was being given the chance to do. Affect another's heart, mind, beliefs. Show them a new world—a better world?

And all of a sudden, I knew who.

Yes.

"It's okay—I mean, I barely know—"

Yes. It will be done.

The voice was gone, and the glow disappeared from the snow. It continued to fall, though, coating the world in a skin of clarity and purity. All of the bad was gone, covered in an ever-growing skin. All of the good was gone, too. The past didn't determine the future.

And that was my gift. The world not as it was, but as it could be.

I rose from the couch and returned to the bedroom. There was enough room on a corner of the bed for me to squeeze in, and I did, feeling the warmth of four sets of lives. Just as I was drifting off, a small voice whispered in my ear.

"Is it Christmas yet, Daddy?"

"It sure is, big guy."

LESLIE FULTON
Hollywood North

It was late by the time Maerwen left the factory. She was tired and hungry. It was cold and snowing. She longed for some soup, a bath and her bed in that order. The last month had been brutal. Work was ramping up, and she was tired of the frenzied bonhomie that was a hallmark of the season. Behind the smiles was a grim determination to get everything done on time. Her boss, a fat man partial to wearing red, was the worst of all. He micromanaged his overworked staff and everybody was feeling the heat.

Maerwen sighed. Her feet ached in her sturdy green leather boots with the turned-up toes. Even the little bells, hung by silver threads around her waist, gave a mournful clink as she walked. They sounded as tired as she felt.

It never used to be this way. Maerwen remembered a time when the human Christmas was a lot of fun. When she first started working at the factory the toys were easy to make—dolls with lustrous hair, trains with blinking lights, and building blocks that transformed into castles with just a little imagination. Now it was electronic games, day in, day out. Maerwen's eyes ached putting the pieces together, and she had never been good at coding.

As she neared the pub across from her apartment, she decided to stop in for a quick drink. A few laughs wouldn't hurt either—she couldn't remember the last time she had smiled spontaneously. All this faux Christmas spirit while punching the clock seven days a week was getting her down.

"Maerwen!" Her friend Santiel waved her over. She was in high spirits, most likely due to the pitcher of mead on the table in front of her.

Maerwen smiled and motioned to the bar. She didn't feel like mead tonight. Something stronger was in order. Perhaps Saerloonian Glowfire, a pale wine that tasted like ripe pears, or Berdruskan Dark, a potent black wine high in alcohol.

Beriadan was working the bar. Maerwen was glad to see him. Not only did he serve a generous pour, he was a sight for sore eyes. He looked like Orlando Bloom, the elf who had made it big in the humans' Hollywood. Maerwen was an avid fan of the Hollywood elves. Cate, Liv, Hugo and Orlando were her favorites. She found it funny that humans thought they were one of them when everybody in Faerie knew differently. The only thing she resented was so many elves had fled the factory to seek their fortune in Hollywood that there weren't enough workers to fill the Christmas shifts.

"What will it be, sweetheart?" Beriadan was a big flirt. It was just what Maerwen needed.

"What's strong and sweet today?" she asked. "I need a real kick."

"Job getting you down?" Beriadan poured her a big glug of Talkana, a potent purple wine made from ram berries. Maerwen nodded her thanks as she downed it in one gulp. He poured her another.

"Maybe I'm just getting too old for this gig," said Maerwen. "I'm definitely losing the Christmas spirit."

"Ho ho ho," said Beriadan flatly. "I hear the old man is pushing you hard this year."

"Tell me about it." She took another sip of her drink, enjoying the slight burn of the ram berries. "We're understaffed and overworked, that's for sure. It seems every elf fair of face has hiked it south to California. Add in a little bedazzlement and the humans fall for it every time. Turn around and there's an elf in another movie."

Beriadan grinned at her. "Well, you're a lovely lady. What are you still doing here?" He turned and looked at himself in the bar's big mirror. "Come to think of it, what am I doing here?" He turned around slowly. "Maerwen..." he said.

She put up a hand to stop him. "Don't even think about it."

"Why not?" Beriadan was excited. He ran a hand through his mop of silvery blond hair. "We're both young, good looking and are ace at shooting arrows. The humans love elves. They'll love *us*."

"But who will make the toys?" Maerwen thought of all the disappointed human children opening their stockings on Christmas morning to find nothing but air. No Nintendo, no computer games, no iPhones, nothing. She could hear their howls of indignation. She could feel salty tears of rage coursing down millions of red, contorted faces.

She shrugged. On second thought, it didn't seem like a bad idea at all. Beriadan, reading her face, could see her hesitation.

"Think of the fame, the money, the cars," he wheedled. "We could be living the good life. We could be partying with Orlando. I betcha he knows how to throw a good one."

Then Maerwen remembered the letter. She had been in charge of opening the Big Guy's fan mail and amid the pleas for faster phones and violent computer games, one handwritten note stood out.

I really don't need anything. I just want to say thank you. I'm sure you work very hard up there, and I've always appreciated it.

She downed her drink and pushed back her chair.

"Nah," she said. "It's not for me. Thanks for the drink, but I've got to get back to work."

LISA T. CRESSWELL
Spell Spinner Christmas

Lindy slipped on the icy pavement and crashed headlong into the cobblestones. The boys surrounded her, still panting from the chase. They waited for Ticker to catch up, unsure what to do with her. Lindy really didn't want to wait around for him. She tried to ignore the stars clouding her vision and the overwhelming pain in her temple. Struggling to stand, Lindy saw the world whirling around her; the wharf, the dirty alley, and the curious collection of ugly street urchins. Ugliest of all, Ticker stepped up and grabbed her by the coat.

"Where's my money, thief?" he shouted, loud enough to hurt Lindy's ears.

"I never took your stupid money!"

Ticker rifled through the pockets of Lindy's jacket.

"Ha! That's a laugh. You've been a thief since the day you were born. What's this?" he said, pulling a long golden chain out of Lindy's blouse. A large pendant dangled on the end of the necklace.

"No!" she cried as he yanked the chain hard enough to break it. He threw the bauble on the pavement and smashed it beneath the heel of his boot.

"Maybe you'll think before you steal from me again, wench," spat Ticker.

A fiery rocket screamed by Ticker's head and exploded with a loud *pop* behind them. Fireworks. Lindy had seen them once at the fair. High above them, another fuse was lit. Lindy gazed up at the Chinese air junk moored at the dock. Someone on the junk, a black-haired Asian boy about Lindy's age, released another rocket. It zipped through the pack of boys, scattering them like rats.

"What are you doing, you crazy Chinaman?" demanded Ticker.

The boy on the junk leaned over the railing, waving another lit rocket.

"I'm blind as a bat so you'd better shove off!"

"He's bleeding bonkers!" yelled Ticker as he dodged another explosion and ran off after his friends.

The boy on the junk cocked his head, listening to the sound of their fading footfalls. He grabbed a rope and swung down to the wharf where Lindy was picking up the pieces of the crushed pendant.

"Ruined...it's all ruined," she muttered, searching the cracks in the cobbles for all the bits.

"What's ruined?"

"Me mum's spell spinner. She needs it. I dunno where I'm gonna find a new one."

"Maybe I can fix it?"

"But you said you were blind."

The boy laughed. "I'm blind, not completely useless. Let me have it." He stripped off his fingerless gloves and held out his hands, waiting. His almond-shaped eyes stared off into nothing.

"It's pretty bad," she said, looking at the crushed metal bits in her hand.

"You're in luck. I specialize in 'pretty bad.' C'mon."

Lindy poured the remnants into his outstretched hands. He felt each piece carefully, assessing the damage.

"It's supposed to go together like this," said Lindy, showing him how the pieces fit in his hand.

"That part is certainly broken, but I have something we can use instead. Come aboard and I'll fix it."

"Um," Lindy hesitated. "We haven't properly met. I'm Lindy Wainswright from Piccadilly."

"Chang Peko from the South China Sea. Call me Peko."

"Nobody comes from the sea, except fish and mermaids," teased Lindy.

"Don't tell my uncle that. We're traders. We've traveled all over. Are you coming?" Peko climbed the rope ladder onto the junk, the spinner parts clutched tight in his fist.

"I'm not sure if I should."

"Are you really a thief?"

"I prefer the term 'wealth liberator,'" said Lindy as she cleaned the mud off her leggings and straightened her jacket. Peko smiled.

"Well, come back tomorrow and I'll have it ready for you."

"All right," said Lindy, already feeling a little remorseful she hadn't climbed aboard. "See you tomorrow... Peko?"

"Yes?"

"Thanks for helping me out, with Ticker and all."

"It was my pleasure," said Peko with a bow.

Lindy hurried home as tiny flakes of snow started to fall. Tomorrow was Christmas. She hoped her mother wouldn't notice the missing spinner.

The next day, Lindy returned to the wharf to see Peko helping several other men loading cargo on the junk. She snuck up behind him and waited until he was alone. She thought she had fooled him, but he spoke first.

"Hello, Lindy. I've got your spinner fixed."

"How did you know it was me?"

"Your footsteps are hesitant, like a bird about to flee," he said. "Oh, Merry Christmas."

Peko had rethreaded the spinner on its chain and now wore it around his neck. He lifted it over his head and handed it to her. She looked it over.

"It's perfect," murmured Lindy in wonder.

"What's it for?"

"It makes magic. Want to see?" she said before she caught herself.

"Yes," he said, looking toward her without focusing on her face.

"I brought you something to say 'thank you.'"

"What is it?"

"I nicked it from the Professor," she said, digging a small box out of her rucksack.

"Lindy, you really shouldn't…"

"I know, Peko. But I wanted you to see London just once. I'll take them back when you're done."

"What are they?" he asked, as she opened the box.

"Spectacles. Put them on."

Lindy handed him a contraption consisting of several lenses on what appeared to be a pair of eye-sized telescopes.

"Spectacles don't work for me."

"Shh, just do as I say." Lindy twisted the spinner and let it fly into the air over Peko's head where it hovered, showering him with a golden light.

"When you help others, your dreams will always come true," she whispered to Peko. The lenses on the spectacles began moving and rearranging themselves, trying one combination, then another. Suddenly, Peko caught his breath in shock.

"I can see! I see you!" he gasped.

Tears leaked from Peko's eyes behind the spectacles, down his cheeks.

"C'mon, Peko. Let's go see London," said Lindy, taking his hand with a smile. "Merry Christmas."

NICK JOHNS
'TWAS THE FIGHT BEFORE CHRISTMAS

I was in trouble. Again.

"Fighting all the time! What is it with him and the twins? I never wanted a reserve anyway. I got along fine for years with my regular crew. What am I supposed to do with him?" his voice boomed.

"You've got to take him," his wife said.

"If he comes with me, I'm rewarding his hooligan behavior."

"And if you don't, you'll never get the job done. Face it, you can't do this shorthanded. It would be a year's work down the drain."

"Oh, I'll manage. Don will be fit. He's a bit bruised and battered, but I'll just adjust the list. That way there would be less calls to make."

"Don't you dare touch that list! It's taken me over a month to get it to the stage it's at now. And Don may be okay, but his brother will be out of action for at least a week. The delivery schedules don't write themselves, you know. They are a finely balanced mechanism. I sometimes think you don't properly appreciate the work that I do. It's all very well for you, getting all the credit, not to mention all the drinks and mince pies, while I slave away here in the background. Hey, where are you going?"

"I'm going to tell him to get ready. He's coming with me."

SO, I was on the team.

The others pretended to ignore me—when he was watching anyway. He'd put me in the front, of course. That way I had to do the most work. No daydreaming for me at the back and just pulling. I had to navigate. The new nav software was useless. Upgrade? I don't think so. It never gave you enough warning.

At the next chimney turn sharp left, then stop on the white roof.

They're all white, genius. It's Lapland.

And every time I stopped suddenly, the others took the chance to run into me. Those horns are sharp, I'm telling you. My ass was like a pincushion by the time we reached Liverpool.

Anyway, the boss was doing the drop when I heard voices.

"Right lads, the NORAD tracker says he's arrived. 'ere we go, just like we planned."

"But Spike, what about the kids?"

"Never mind about that."

"But Spike, 'e's a right big bloke…"

"He's an old man. Do you want to be in this gang or not? Just do it!"

"But Spike, 'e moves proper fast…"

"That's what the net's for, stupid! He gets tangled up, we grab the sack and leg it. Shh. 'ere we go. Got 'im!"

I looked down into the street and saw the boss, flailing about, caught up and bellowing like a beached walrus. They hit him on the head with a stick, and he went quiet. The three lads started stuffing the presents he'd dropped back into the sack.

Behind me the others were in an uproar.

"What shall we do now?" snickered Cupid.

"I could run for help," said Dasher

"Zis is all your fault. If you hadn't landed here, ve vouldn't be in zis mess…" It was Donner, of course. Still sore about the number I'd done on him and Blitzen.

I'd had enough of their whining. I bit through the traces and leaped off the roof.

I landed square on top of the first guy, He lay stunned in a big heap in the dirty snow.

I spun around and kicked at the next guy. Caught him right in the gut. He doubled over and lay there, gasping and retching.

The third guy had a knife.

I backed up and looked at him. Eyes like a ferret and a stupid kiss-curl haircut. This must be Spike.

"Hi Spike. My name's Rudy," I said.

He just stopped, like he'd been turned to stone.

"A talking reindeer bothers you? That's not even the start of your problems, pal. I'm a fourteen-point buck and weigh just shy of four hundred pounds. My feet are superbly adapted for fighting in the snow. This red nose, you see. It ain't jam. I fight…a lot."

Spike shivered, and I didn't think it was from the cold. He backed up slowly.

I lowered my head slightly, and the streetlights caught the glistening frost on my antlers.

"And you've got, what? One knife? You've got to ask yourself one question: Do I feel lucky? Well, do ya, punk?"

I always wanted to say that line.

I put my head back and gave a full-throated bellow. The windows rattled. Spike turned and ran.

The old man leaned on my neck as I helped him back to the sled.

"Next year, Boss, how about I come along anyway? Looks like you could use the protection."

S.R. BETLER
The Wild Hunters

The baying of the hounds was so loud that Osgar could feel it thundering through his bones. Father had warned him to stay in bed, especially this night, but Father's snoring was loud and uninterrupted. There was no reason he'd have to know.

The frigid winter air gave him pause, but with a sharp inhale, he braved the bare wood that nipped through his socks. What was left of the Yule fire had been reduced to embers, but it was enough to guide his way.

The baying outside had been joined by a thudding so monstrous that even the earth quaked. Still, his parents slept soundly. Osgar minded the squeaky hinges as he opened the door just enough for him to squeeze through.

Outside, the twilight had been painted white from the boughs of the trees to the distant rolling hills. Fat snowflakes broke from the clouds and pirouetted down like millions of dancers—sometimes twirling, sometimes redirected by the breeze. Though his breath emerged in wisps, Osgar was otherwise warm, even in his nightwear.

In the distance, a consort of men were just cresting a hill, their colossal horses kicking up a flurry of snow as they galloped, creating a cloud of white in their wake. They were massive and imposing, as far away as they were. The men were all bearded and decked out in furs—some with horns, all with weapons. Muscles rippled through the flanks of the steeds, and their armor clanked and jangled like a war song.

As they drew closer, the hoof-beats became deafening, and every ounce of Osgar vibrated with the force. The leader looked down on him as they passed. There was a harshness in his white-blue eye, and a patch over the other. Despite that, he inclined his graying head by way of greeting, and Osgar returned the gesture. None of the other hunters paid him any mind. Their eyes were focused forward, faces tense, lips drawn. The last man in their convoy, upon seeing Osgar, drew back on his reins. His steed protested the sudden stop, prancing sideways and snorting its disapproval.

Osgar fought to keep his composure as he looked up at the endless figure. The hunter was imposing, no doubt about that, but not in a way that wrought fright. He was impressive, admirable even, and at that moment, with the hunter eclipsing the sky, Osgar realized a sudden desire to be like him.

Everything about the hunter was dark—from his black eyes to his braided beard to the horse that bore him. Even so, there was a warmth in his eyes, and his voice was patient as he demanded, "What's your name, boy?"

It took a moment for Osgar to remember his voice.

"Ansehelm Osgar Leutwin Gero Borchardt." He rattled it off as he'd been taught. Remembering his manners, as an afterthought, he added, "Sir."

"*Rufname?*"

"Osgar."

"Tell me, can you hunt, Osgar?"

"Yes." Osgar pondered the merits of exaggerating. Not lying, per se, but inflating the truth. Something about the stranger implied that wouldn't be wise, so he admitted, "Well, small game. Hares and the like."

The hunter unleashed a roar of laughter, and his steed whinnied along as if he were in on the joke.

"This is no hare we're after."

His instincts warned him that he was sure not to like the answer, but Osgar asked anyway. "What is it you're hunting?"

"A fearsome predator with the body of a wolf and the mind of a man. His howl can break a mortal, and his words can tear down cities. He is a worthy foe, not to be taken lightly, for sure."

Osgar looked down at his small hands, every bit as delicate as a woman's, despite the wood splitting and trapping. He had always considered himself on the verge of manhood, but now, he was unsure. What sort of man would it take to conquer the Monster of the River Ván?

"What happens if you don't catch him?" Osgar asked, looking back up at the hunter.

"He'll destroy the world."

"And if you do?"

"All of Valhalla will hold a feast in our honor." The hunter paused, and a softness came to his features as he leaned closer. "So, I ask you again: can you hunt?"

Osgar looked at his hands again, this time balling them into fists. Such an obvious question, with an equally obvious answer, but something kept him from giving it.

Instead, he said, "You never told me your name."

The hunter grunted and seemed to mull over the idea. Beneath him, his steed hooved the ground and snorted impatiently.

Finally, the hunter acquiesced. "I am Anselhelm Badulf Leutwin Borchardt."

"Badulf?" Osgar said, rolling the name off his tongue. It was familiar. He was sure his father had used it before, in the story of a great man Osgar had never met, gone before his time. The rest of the name was unmistakable.

"You may call me 'sir.'"

"Of course, sir. I can't hunt, not yet anyway, but I'm a quick study."

"Is that so?"

Badulf's features hardened as he appeared to weigh Osgar's merit, so the boy stuck his chest out and did his best to look worthy.

In the distance, a horn bellowed a resounding, baleful note, and then others took up the call. The sound drew Badulf's attention, and he reached one strong, leathery hand out to Osgar.

"The Hunt is nigh. Climb up, and I'll show you the way."

Osgar hesitated. For two winters, since he had first fallen ill, his father had warned him against wandering at night, especially during Yule. Tomorrow, his father would find what he left behind—the shell of a human and a few footprints in the snow—and know his betrayal.

"To join the Wild Hunt is a great honor. He will understand," Badulf whispered.

Osgar nodded and took his place on the back of the steed, holding tight as it galloped away from the rising sun.

JENNIFER GARRETT
A CHRISTMAS CHANGE

Gemma put down the phone receiver and glared at her husband, Alex. "That's the last one. None of our three children will be home for Christmas." She frowned as she took in the almost naked Christmas tree, adorned only with lights so far, while pine boughs garnished the nearby banister.

Alex took her hands into his. "Stop. Let's do it. We've talked about it for years. The two of us should go away for Christmas."

Gemma shifted in her seat. "Only us? What about Christmas Eve dinner, Christmas morning breakfast? What if one of the kids needs us?"

Alex chuckled. "They can text or call us, like everyone else. This is just what we need. The kids will have their fun, and we can have ours."

"I… I… I don't know. It doesn't feel right. We should be here."

Alex let out a deep sigh. "It doesn't feel right because we are so caught up in the routine hustle and bustle of the holidays from Thanksgiving until January that we forget about us. This is a gift. Let's grab it."

The myriad boxes filled with decorations collected over the twenty-five years they had been together caught her attention. Her eyes misted. "Can we still make the place festive, even if we decide to go?"

The corners of his mouth turned up, forming a grin. "Of course. And I've got the perfect retreat in mind. I'm gonna keep it a secret—my gift to you. Now help me decorate the tree. We need to get in the spirit. And let's make some hot chocolate. Our holiday celebration may be a little different this year, but it's still Christmas."

Gemma bounded to her feet. "Hot chocolate for two coming right up. You know? This is gonna be so much fun."

"SHOULDN'T YOU tell me where we're going now? Our departure is tomorrow."

Alex shook his head. "Not quite yet. I'll tell you on the plane. But count on it being cold. Like winter should be."

Gemma poked her head from behind the closet door, her arms full of sweaters. "Will this be enough?"

"More than enough," he assured her. "Oh, well… I guess I'll tell you." Alex pulled out a magazine from his back pocket, flipped through the pages, then stopped, and handed it over to Gemma.

She squealed. "Really? I can't wait!" Gemma jumped into his arms, tackling him to the bed.

"Now that's the kind of appreciation I can get in line with. Let our Christmas vacation begin," he said, as he returned her kiss.

GEMMA'S BOOTS crunched the packed snow as she approached the rustic cabin ahead of her, smoke billowing from the chimney. The surrounding thick tree branches hid in part the small structure, while Christmas lights beckoned through the midnight sky, illuminating the path toward her bed for the night.

"That's the last of the luggage," Alex said as he stomped the snow from his boots and shut the door behind him. "Wow, take a look at that spread."

"Isn't it great? Come join me for a picnic feast by the fire," Gemma said, making herself comfortable, patting the space beside her.

"Tomorrow," he said, gathering some cushions around him, "we'll board a train and head toward the Northern Lights. There'll be more food, drinks, wildlife, and views unmatched anywhere else on Earth."

"But first we'll explore Fairbanks?" Gemma asked before biting into an apple. "I'm reading up on their Christmas traditions. Everyone contributes to stockings for needy children, and maybe we can catch one of the seasonal plays also."

"As long as we don't miss our train," Alex said. "More wine?"

"*Mmm*, yes. I think we should take a solo trip every Christmas," she said, nuzzling her head onto Alex's shoulder.

"LOOK—A MOOSE," Alex shouted, as he raced to the porch, abandoning his breakfast in favor of his camera. Gemma grabbed her robe and rushed to catch a glimpse as the beast took its time traipsing through the light falling snow. Time seemed to pause as the giant animal met their gazes, then meandered on his way.

"I could get used to this," Alex said.

"LET'S STOP here and take a quick look around before boarding the train," Gemma said.

Alex threw the gear shift into Park. "Sorry, honey. Don't have that much time. The train's about to leave. Maybe on the way back. Help me grab the luggage, and we can explore from the train."

The ride provided hours to observe the local wildlife. Snow decorated the landscape, piled high in pristine mounds. The *clickety-clack* rhythm of the train slowed as they neared the station. Gemma stared out the window in awe at the dogsled team tethered there, complete with bells and red kerchiefs. She laughed. "Can you imagine us in one of those things?"

"Well, yes, actually I could," Alex said with a smirk.

Gemma's mouth dropped. "You didn't."

"I did."

Thirty minutes later, a meet and greet done with the dogs, the sled departed—blankets, hot drinks, and guide in tow—traveling deep into the woods, their destination a secluded heated tent.

Gemma met Alex's gaze as the evening's show presented an array of colors that penetrated the sky, providing a unique display of unparalleled hues and lights. "I can't believe this trip you planned, just for us. I feel so special." Her eyes welled with tears.

He pulled her chin even with his own. "You *are* special. Not even this spectacular aurora shines brighter than you." Their lips brushed in a tender kiss. "You know what? We should experience another event during this dazzling display."

"What's that?" she whispered. "I can't imagine anything else."

"Let me show you how much I love you and why this Christmas—and the next and the one after that and for all the years to come—I'll be there with you. Merry Christmas, Gemma."

A tear fell from her cheek. And, hand in hand, they walked into their tent.

BETH AVERY
The Town Beneath the Lake

The cold is so sharp I can feel it outlining my sinuses when I breathe in. It's an exceptionally clear night, and the dark mountains on the horizon provide a welcome boundary between the blackness of the immense expanse of ice and the blackness of the star-interrupted sky. Before I slide onto the ice, I test my laces one last time. I'm too old to take a hard fall without risking a broken bone, and I have no intention of being found frozen like a popsicle on Christmas morning. This is the first time I will be making this trip alone. For sixty years, Etta and I met on Christmas Eve to make this journey.

We were only twelve for that initial midnight skate. Back then, we were still smarting from the loss of our town in the valley. When the final petition for the big dam went through, our families lost. The year the lake was filled and froze, we arranged to sneak out the night before Christmas to lie on the ice above our old homes and talk about the beautiful Christmas light competitions our community used to have. Our old neighbors had scattered when the town was condemned. Some found homes along the side of the lake, but many simply moved far away from the little town in the valley.

My mother kept saying it wasn't so bad, but Etta and I were heartbroken. All the secret hiding places and play areas of our childhood rested beneath fifty feet of water. That first midnight skate, we were mournful. We silently slid over the ice using the radio tower and the new wharf as markers to help us find the part of the lake that covered our old homes. Once there, we stretched out with our cheeks against the ice, peering down and trying to believe we could make out the shapes of the buildings we knew had to be down there.

We weren't really expecting to see anything. We were just two maudlin girls creating a ritual to deal with the first big loss of our lives. We probably squinted at the lights shining from the depths for several minutes before Etta whispered, "Do you see that, Jane?"

"The lights?" I whispered.

"Are they ghosts?" Etta quavered.

We stared for a long time before I answered. "I think…I think it's the Walden house," I said. "Look, see how it makes a square of green with a square of red and then a star in white? That's just how the Waldens always did their lights."

We were quiet then, half frozen in fear and wonder, acutely aware that we were two small bodies out on a great field of ice above a tiny drowned town that appeared to still be living. We finally summoned up the courage to stand up, and then we skated furiously and frantically for the shore. I fell a few times, but Etta did not stop until she was back on solid ground.

We had a whole year to think about what had happened that night before Christmas came around again. In that year, my mother received news that Grandfather Walden had died a few weeks before our first skate. We had been a close-knit community, so it grieved her that she did not learn of his death until after his funeral. When another elderly member of our old town died that year, she made sure we went to pay our respects. We were afraid to go, but our parents reminded us that Mr. Stark had been a kind librarian who had always given the children gifts on Christmas and took special care to decorate the library for the holidays.

Etta and I argued long and hard about whether we were going back out the next Christmas Eve. A year older, we had decided that we had imagined the lights. It became a rite of passage to prove we were not babies, and we bravely went out above the ice and looked down again.

It was harder the second time. I was so scared I thought I was going to be sick. Etta clutched my hand as we glided out to the center of the lake. We didn't lie down this time. We both stared down, poised to flee if any ghostly faces floated up to greet us. I almost bolted when I saw the familiar pattern of the Walden Christmas lights, but Etta grabbed my arm.

"Look," she said.

I peered and saw another set of lights a goodly distance from the Walden house. "It's where the library would be," I said.

She nodded.

We didn't run this time. We watched peacefully, and suddenly our love for our lost home didn't seem so childish. We were not the only ones who thought it had been heaven on earth.

The skate was less scary after that. Some years there weren't any new homes lit up; some years there were three or four. This year I skate out alone, but Etta promised she would put up a blue star for me on her house. If she keeps her promise, it won't feel so bad to be the last person alive who once lived in Ruhetal.

LARA HAYS
THE TALISMAN

"Do you know what today is, boy?"

The day I became a pirate, I thought darkly. But I knew that was not the answer the pirate captain wanted. "No, sir."

"Where's Johnny boy?"

Amid a chorus of heckles, a boy came forward. I knew it was wrong to stare, but I couldn't take my eyes off the teenager shuffling forward. He was pale. Impossibly pale. Tall and lanky. He was older than me—seventeen or eighteen. And his eyes were pink. The color would've been pretty in a sunset, but eyes were not meant to be that color. I recoiled instinctively.

As the boy approached the captain, his sickly pink eyes widened a fraction and his hands flexed.

"What day is it, Johnny boy?" the captain asked.

Johnny looked down. "Christmas, sir."

There was a flash of movement and a sickening crack. I couldn't believe what I saw. Without any provocation, the captain had backhanded the boy. Johnny didn't flinch or cry out. He just wiped the blood from his lip.

The captain beamed at me. "Normally, we only allow Johnny to take a punch a day. But seein' as it's Christmas, I removed the limits."

A tawny man I knew to be the gunner grabbed Johnny by the shoulder and sunk a fist deep in his gut. Another pirate landed another punch. Then another. In a matter of seconds, Johnny was prostrate, seven or eight pirates on top of him.

When they were done, Johnny moaned and struggled to his feet. He was holding his side, and his face was bleeding.

The captain looked at me. "Have a turn. It's my Christmas gift to the crew. And yer one of us now."

I stood agape.

The captain shifted his weight and rested a hand on the hilt of his sword. "I might find it insulting if you don't accept my gift."

Did I really have to hit this boy? What would they do to me if I didn't?

A man cleared his throat and stepped forward. He was round and ruddy with a flaxen beard. His shoulders were stooped, and his voice was soft. "Pardon me, Captain, but the boy needs time. It weren't three hours ago that he saw his entire crew killed."

The captain let out a breath. "The lad will open his gift later. Let's work on putting the new cargo away."

The crew dissipated, even Johnny, leaving me alone with the soft-spoken pirate.

He held out his hand to me. "Simon Skidmore."

I hesitated, then shook it. "Nicholas Holladay."

Skidmore looked me up and down. With an avuncular tone, he said, "Lose your boots. You'll be steadier in the ratlines."

I nodded. "Thanks for…" I gestured broadly, not sure how to phrase my thoughts. "Am I really going to have to hit that boy?"

Skidmore shrugged. "Plenty of people do."

"Do you?"

Skidmore shook his head then shifted his attention to the sails. "We've got a heavin' line. Help me tack it."

"Is this what Christmas is always like?" I looked at Johnny's blood on the deck.

"What was Christmas like for you?"

I grabbed the line and shrugged. "Begging got a bit better this time of year. Meat pies and maybe even a pastry. Never got a present, though. Never gave one neither. Beating Johnny…that don't seem like a very good gift. Leastways not for him."

"That's why I don't hit him," Skidmore said.

AS THE Christmas celebration wound down, the captain stood, Johnny at his side. "The night's slipping away. Has everyone received their Christmas gift?"

A few pirates bellowed that they hadn't hit Johnny yet.

The captain called them forward. He also summoned me. "Who'll be first?"

I stepped forward.

"Young Mr. Holladay." The captain smiled.

I pressed my lips together, fisted my hands, then turned and stood in front of Johnny. "I'd like to give Johnny a Christmas gift," I said, my voice thin. "Hit me instead of him."

I TOOK eight punches. Johnny took four. We sat in a hidden corner of the gun deck mopping our wounds and bragging up our battle scars.

Then Johnny grew serious. "I ain't never had no one stand up for me like that."

I could feel blood pumping into my cheeks. I didn't say anything.

"No one," Johnny said again, emphasizing his words. "Even me own mum put me out. Some nuns took care of me for a while, but then I got too old. I always heard anyone could find a home with pirates. You see slaves with skin black as night, but I guess there's no place for someone with skin white like mine."

"It shouldn't matter," I muttered angrily, thinking of what my mother went through because of the color of her skin.

"You shouldn't've stood up for me. A stunt like that can get you killed."

I shook my head. "This may have been the first time someone's stood up for you, but it won't be the last."

He sighed. "I just hate being me. I don't want to be Johnny. I don't want to be white. If I could have a real Christmas wish, that's what I'd wish for."

"You're in luck," I said smugly. "I'm in the business of granting Christmas wishes. From this day on you'll be known as Jack. And you won't be white anymore. You'll be Black Jack—the meanest pirate in the Spanish Main. A man would have to be a git to gamble with a man named Black Jack."

The boy beamed. "Black Jack. I like it." He removed something from around his neck. "Hold out your hand."

I did as he asked, and he dropped a golden crucifix on a chain in my palm. "One of the nuns gave me this to help protect me. A talisman. I don't think I need it anymore."

"I can't take this." I moved to give it back.

Black Jack held up his hands. "I've never had a friend to give a present to."

I draped the chain around my neck. "No one's ever given me a Christmas present before."

"I guess this means we're friends," Jack said, his swollen lips stretching into a smile.

"Yeah." I grinned. "I guess it does."

MARY MACFARLANE
I'll Be Home for Christmas

Emily pressed her nose against the cold windowpane until her breath fogged up her view of the wintery dark world outside. It was still and quiet except for the occasional breeze that blew some of the snow off the lighted lamppost in the front yard. No sign of anyone coming up the driveway. Heaving a sigh, she swiped the glass clean with a pudgy fist and bounded down the stool, brown pigtails bouncing. She grabbed her stuffed elephant and hugged it tightly to her chest.

"Mommy, do you believe in Santa?"

Nadine set down the popcorn string she was working on and smiled a tired smile at her five-year-old daughter.

"Do *you* believe in Santa?"

Emily thought about it a minute. "Paul says he isn't real. He says that daddies pretend to be Santa and that the mailman eats all of Santa's letters for breakfast."

"And what does Emily think?"

"I want Santa to be real," she said wistfully as she hopped back up the stool to stare out the window. "He has to be real."

Nadine went back to stringing on the popcorn kernels. Life hadn't been easy since her husband had disappeared in the terrible blizzard last year. They had managed to scrape by so far, but finances were getting tighter all the time, and she really didn't want to have to search for a full-time job outside of the home. She didn't want Emily to be just another daycare kid.

Elvis started crooning, "I'll Be Home for Christmas" on the record player. Tears welled up in her eyes. Tom would never be coming home for Christmas again. Quickly, she dabbed her eyes with the sleeve of her sweater and stole a glance at Emily. Thankfully the little girl was still occupied gazing out the window.

"Good kids get what they asked Santa for, right Mommy?"

"Yes, darling."

"Good. I was especially good this year!"

"Yes, you were, darling. I'm sure Santa made Ellie a nice sweater."

A suppressed giggle came from the window.

"Emily, why do you keep looking out the window? Come and help Mommy finish decorating for Santa."

The brown pigtails shook in a vigorous *no*. "I have to keep watching!"

"Watching for what, sweetie?" Another suppressed giggle. Nadine shook her head and smiled again as she tied off the end of the string. It would be time for bed soon and the few measly presents she had managed to put together from "Santa" would go under the Charlie Brown tree. She had spent hours at night knitting the little cardigan for Ellie, her stuffed elephant.

The popcorn was strung across the mantel, and the cookies and milk were set on the table—they were ready for Christmas. Nadine rolled her shoulders in a stretch and crossed over to the window to wrap her arms around her daughter.

"Bedtime, Emily," she whispered. The little girl didn't budge from her perch. "Bedtime, Emily!" she said a little louder.

"Shh!" Emily put a finger over her lips, head tilted as her young ears picked up some sound Nadine couldn't hear. Then it came, softly at first, then gradually louder. The jingle of bells. What was this? Some kind neighbor helping make their Christmas magical?

She gasped as an over-laden sleigh hauled by eight caribou settled onto their driveway. In the driver seat sat a rather obese man in a red fur coat who turned and waved at them. Out of the sleigh tumbled a stick-figure of a man.

"Daddy!" Emily shrieked. Jumping down from her stool, she scampered to the front door and threw it open. Dashing out across the lawn, arms outstretched, she tumbled into the waiting arms of the man. Nadine was still in too much shock to move. She was sure her eyes were playing tricks on her, but eventually she found her way outside where she could see for herself who this really was.

"Tom?"

The face that glanced up was gaunt, gristly, and hardened, but the blue eyes that twinkled underneath were unmistakable.

"Tom!" Nadine joined the heap in the snow, her laughter bubbling through her tears of happiness as Tom embraced wife and daughter for the first time in a year.

The old man in the sleigh watched with a smile glowing on his wrinkled cheeks, quite forgotten and happy to have it so. Slapping the caribou with the reigns, he clucked his tongue and backed the loaded vehicle out of the driveway. As the sleigh began to rise into the air, he cast his eyes on the weathered sheet of notebook paper in his hand:

Deer Santa Claz,

I now I was a good girl but I dont want any toys. Pleas find my daddy. We misss him lots. I want Mommy to laf agin. We need my daddy for Krismas. Thank yoo!

Hugs and kisses,
Emily

ERIC MARTELL
Wally, the Penguin Who Could Fly

For as long as he could remember, Wally wanted to fly. At dinner, he told his mom and dad about the planes that had passed overhead that day, appearing as nothing but black dots on one horizon and then disappearing on the other, the only sign of their passage a trail of clouds in the sky. Wally thrilled at the sight of the wings and tail making the outline of a giant bird in the sky, and would waddle around excitedly, chirping and squawking loudly enough to wake up the whole flock.

"But Wally," his dad said. "You're a penguin. And penguins can't fly."
"Wally," his mom said. "Eat your fish. They're getting warm."
"Stop squawking, Wally," his neighbors said. "We need to sleep!"
So Wally learned not to run around excitedly and squawk and chirp every time he saw a plane. But he didn't stop dreaming of soaring through the air.

One night, the snow glowing in the light of a full moon, Wally saw something different flying through the sky. It wasn't a bird. It wasn't a plane. There was a red light that winked in and out and nine flying animals, the likes of which he'd never seen, pulling a large sled behind them. He didn't hear chirping or squawking but instead a faint "Ho, ho, ho!" calling down from above.

From that day on, Wally was obsessed not just with flying but also the strange red light that appeared in the sky just once a year.

One day while out fishing, Wally got separated from his family. A strong current pulled him north and his little wings weren't big enough to make it back to shore. So he sailed away from his home and his parents and the only world he'd ever known.

But the oceans were full of fish, and he floated easily on the water, and after many days, the current pulled him close to land. The ground was rocky, and the beach was full of other birds of all shapes and sizes, birds who could fly and chirp and tweet. Wally asked these birds if they'd ever seen the red light in the sky, but most of them were too young and too interested in cracking open shells on the ground to answer.

A wise, old albatross knew what he was talking about. "The light you seek comes from the north, and it belongs to a very special animal named Rudolph. He doesn't have wings, but can fly all around the world in a single night. It will be a long journey, but if you seek him, follow the light of the North Star until it is directly over your head."

Wally thanked the bird and set off to the north, marking off the distance a foot at a time with his short legs, waddling over rocks and hills and through valleys. He swam across rivers and splashed in the ocean.

The weather grew warmer, and he wasn't sure if he'd be able to continue. He dreamt of the red light in the sky and persevered until it began cooling off again. He met thousands of birds and marveled at their wings, wishing as he did every day, that he could fly.

Finally, he started to see ice and snow everywhere he went, and the world began to remind him of the home he'd left so far behind him. He still hadn't found the red light in the sky, though the North Star was nearly overhead, and he realized that he missed his mom and his dad and his grumpy neighbors.

One cloudy night, he plopped himself down on a snowbank and cried. Wally was tired. He was lonely. And he knew he'd never fly. He just wanted to go home. Because his eyes were closed, he didn't see the man approaching him. But he felt the arm around his shoulders and heard a warm voice. "Don't be sad, Wally. You're not alone anymore."

Wiping the tears from his eyes with one flipper, Wally looked up at the man who was speaking. He was dressed all in red, and had a thick white beard to keep him warm on a cold night such as this. "How…how did you know my name?"

"I know everyone's name. And I know what you're here for. Come, let me carry you."

The big man in red picked Wally up and carried him to his house, a large cottage next to an even bigger barn. Knowing that Wally wouldn't be happy wrapped up next to a fire, he brought him to the barn to introduce him to his team. The reindeer were excited to see him—there weren't many people in Antarctica to deliver presents to, and they hadn't met that many penguins. They were all friendly, but none more than the one he'd followed from the other end of the world.

Rudolph knew what it was like to want something everyone else said was impossible, and he spent hours with the penguin who'd traveled so far, sharing stories and talking about the many places they'd visited. As they talked, the man in the red suit brought Wally a bucket of fish.

Rudolph excused himself to talk to the man. When they came back, the man had a serious look on his face.

"Wally, you've arrived on a very busy day for us. Tomorrow night is Christmas Eve, and my reindeer and I need to leave soon to bring gifts to people all over the world."

Wally hung his head. His new friend was going to leave, and as exciting as it was to have finally met him, he didn't know if he'd be able to make the long walk home.

The man in the red suit knelt down next to Wally and put his hand on his flipper. "Wally, would you like to come with us? We can fly you home."

He traveled the world with the reindeer and his new friend, and as they flew back toward his home, the red light from Rudolph's nose guided them through a snowstorm, bringing them in for a safe landing in front of his mom, his dad, and his squawking neighbors, who excitedly circled around Wally, the penguin who could fly.

MARISSA AMES
Rebirth in Bethlehem

Mariam pressed against the sandstone wall and waited in the darkness. Soldiers marched past, their spiked sandals scraping the dry road. She pulled her scarf up over her head.

Men knew her kind on sight. Righteous women did not roam the streets of David's City past midnight in tattered robes and unshod feet. Women with homes were tucked safely inside right now.

Maybe the soldiers would ignore her. Maybe they would have some decency tonight. The Romans patrolled the growing crowds, as travelers sought lodging. Maybe they would let her pass.

Mariam pulled her robes tight around her as the spring wind blew in from the hills. Candles flickered above her. Chatter subsided as residents tugged on ropes, dropping thin carpets over the windows and blocking out the breeze.

Mariam left her refuge.

Travelers lined the streets fourfold. Just days ago, they crammed their families into the inns. Tonight, they slept on the road. When they saw her, they threw crushed figs. Her kinfolk knew what she was. Daughter of the poor, she earned her bread the only way she knew. Irredeemable, they called her. Harlot, hopeless and damned.

She tented her scarf over her head and sprinted to another building.

Inside, publicans worked by candlelight, taxing per decree of Caesar. Though the travelers would leave once taxed, the Romans remained. They claimed they kept the peace. More often, they tormented the Jews, taking from them as they did within Rome.

The Messiah was supposed to redeem them from injustice such as this.

Mariam scoffed at the thought.

Moses had not been the Messiah. Nor had this Messiah come during Jerusalem's capture by Assyria or by Babylon. Nor during Ptolemy's reign, and not now, during Herod's. For millennia, the priests promised redemption by a Messiah.

Mariam decided long ago that the Messiah was not real and would not come. If he did, he would not come for her. Salvation came for those who paid generous tithes at the temple. Not for the poor who could only offer a crust of bread.

Her stomach growled. Mariam wrapped her scarf tighter and ascended the streets toward the hills. She passed the natural caves at the edge of town.

Other meek and poor people gathered above the city. Tonight, they kept vigil over the flocks. Ewes often foundered during birthing, and shepherds could save both ewe and lamb. They exchanged watch, some sleeping, and others alert for the sounds of distressed ewes.

They smiled, hailed her, and offered a place by the fire. She accepted a crust of old bread, leaned back, and gazed at the sky.

"It's new," they said as she beheld a star brighter than the fullest moon. Downhill, the walls of Bethlehem reflected the light.

As Mariam stared, the star brightened. It grew nearer to the earth. Shepherds cried out in fear. Mariam toppled forward, pressing her forehead to the sand and clenching her crust of bread.

"Fear not," a voice pulsed through the air. The rocks and trees echoed the words.

Mariam looked up.

A man stood in the air, dressed in luminescent white.

The shepherds raised their draped heads, staring and whispering, "*Adonai.*"

The man's words reverberated into Mariam's breast. He spoke of good tidings and great joy, unto all people. He said, "For unto you is born this day in the city of David a Savior, which is Christ the Lord. And this shall be a sign unto you; Ye shall find the babe wrapped in swaddling clothes, lying in a manger."

A Savior? Another claim to the Messiah?

The shepherds exclaimed in wonder and pointed at the sky.

"Glory to God," new and powerful voices said around them. "Glory to God in the highest, and on earth peace, good will toward men."

The sky filled with men and women, all dressed in luminescent white. Beautiful, perfect beings that made her ashamed of her tattered clothing and stained soul…yet hopeful at the same time. Mariam rose to her feet.

The shepherds rose around her.

Singing praises to God, the shining people retreated into the night sky. The light dimmed, leaving the shepherds in simple starlight, afraid to speak.

One young boy started down the hill. Other shepherds followed. Mariam started forward, then stopped. The angels had told the righteous shepherds to go into Bethlehem. Not her.

A kindly old shepherd tugged on her sleeve. "Unto all men," he said in a wavering voice still thick with awe. "And all women. Will you argue with God's messengers?"

More shepherds descended the hill, leaving only enough people to watch the birthing ewes. They promised to bring word of what they found.

The angels had said the Messiah would be in a cave, not a temple or by Rachel's Tomb. Not surrounded by riches.

As they passed into the upper city, where the caves held livestock, they heard a little cry.

Mariam stopped.

A lamb bleated, its voice soft and mewing.

She walked again.

This time, she heard the cry of a new baby who had just found his own voice. She slowly stepped into the cave to see two adults in the darkness. A woman, barely out of adolescence, lifted a baby from a manger and held him to her breast.

The mother looked up in alarm. Giving the shepherds a nervous smile, she said, "Will you come in?" Slowly and hesitantly, the shepherds accepted the offer. She brought the child down from his breast and lifted a corner of cloth. Shyly, she smiled up at the shepherds.

Mariam's mouth went dry as she beheld the humble parents. They wore tattered robes, as she did, dirty from travel. Their feet were shod with sandals that were broken and tied together. They looked hungry.

Mariam still clenched the crust of bread. She took a timid step toward the mother and extended her hand. "It's all I have to offer," she whispered, watching her own dirty feet.

The mother's fair hand met hers. "It's enough," she whispered back.

SARA DANIELL
Snowed In

Roars of anger erupted throughout the airport for the sixth time in the past hour. Flights were being delayed one after another because of a huge blizzard that hit the east coast this morning. I'd be spending my Christmas here.

I left Mom a voicemail letting her know what was going on and then went to find coffee. I figured I would need some fuel to keep me going so I could send out some work emails while I was stranded. I found a Starbucks and rolled my bag behind me into the line. I rubbed my tired eyes as the line inched forward.

I stared at the menu trying to figure out what I wanted, when I felt someone tap me on my shoulder. I turned to see a man with dark eyes and a sleepy smile. "Can I help you?" I asked.

He pointed toward the counter. "It's your turn."

"Huh?"

He chuckled lightly. "To order coffee. You're in line to order."

"Oh my god." I slapped my forehead. "I swear, I'm sleepwalking. I was just distracted I guess." I turned and moved to the counter. "Peppermint Mocha Grande with an extra shot of espresso. No, make it two shots."

The girl behind the counter rang me up, and I handed her my card. She grabbed a cup and a Sharpie. "Name?"

"Nora Baker."

She nodded, slid the cup to the person to her left, and mumbled, "Next."

I went down to the end of the counter and waited. I checked my phone, but there were no calls or texts from Mom. She probably thought I was lying and trying to bail on coming home. I slid my phone into my back jean pocket when my name was called. I took the coffee and sat down at the only vacant table.

I opened my bag and pulled my laptop out. I set it on the table and looked to my right where I saw the guy that was behind me in line. He was sipping his coffee, just standing there. He looked so tired, and I felt bad that I took the last table. When he saw me looking at him, I smiled and waved him over.

He walked over and sat down across from me. "Are you sure you don't mind? I don't want to be a bother."

"I could have missed my chance at coffee if it weren't for you. It's the least I could do."

"Well, thank you."

I smiled and opened my laptop. *Shit.* It was dead, and all the nearby outlets were taken. I closed it and huffed.

"The news says this blizzard is worse than the one that hit in 1993."

"Just my luck."

He tilted his head to the side a little. "What do you mean?"

I took a sip of my coffee and set it back down on the table, clasping both hands around its warmth. I tapped my index finger on the cup and shrugged. "Christmas has its way of rearing its ugly head every year. Christmas doesn't agree with me. Ever."

He sat up straight and laughed. "Oh, come on, Nora. Christmas is the best time of year."

"That's what they want you to believe. How do you know my name?"

He pointed to my cup. "It's right there."

I looked at his cup and saw "Sean" written on it. I blushed. "Oh. Right."

His smile widened. "So, where are you headed?"

"Maine."

He took off his jacket and laid it on the back of his chair. "What's in Maine?"

I hesitated, unsure if I should unveil such deep things to a complete stranger. But Sean seemed nice, and it wasn't like I'd ever see him again after this snowed-in fiasco, so if he labeled me a crazy lady it wouldn't matter. It'd be good to have someone to vent to.

"My father is dying of liver cancer. I haven't seen or spoken to him in four years."

His forehead creased, and his smile fell. "Oh. I'm so sorry."

"He's a selfish man, more concerned with his possessions than his own daughter, but I guess when you're on your deathbed you feel the need to make amends. Everyone deserves the chance to make things right." I took a deep breath and let it out. I sat up in my chair and took a drink. "What about you, Sean? Where are you headed?"

His eyes fell to his cup of coffee before meeting mine again. "To meet my son."

I smiled. "A new father? Congratulations! Did this storm cause you to miss his birth?"

He shook his head, and his frown deepened. "No, my pride and selfishness caused me to miss his birth eight years ago."

"Damn. I'm sorry. I shouldn't have…" I stopped for lack of anything better to say.

He laughed sadly and waved his hand. "Don't be. You didn't know." He took a drink and smiled a little. "Looks like we're both trying to make amends this Christmas."

"It appears we are."

"Can I ask you something, and if you're not comfortable answering, just tell me."

"Sure."

"If your father wasn't dying and he asked to see you, would you have gone?"

I chewed on the inside of my cheek as I thought. "Honestly, I don't know. Maybe. I've wanted my whole life to be the daughter my parents tried to raise, but I never could live up to their expectations. I'm the daughter with the gypsy-soul. I'd like to think that I would, because regardless of their lack of compassion and love for money, I still love them and know they love me too."

"I hope my son feels that way." He lifted his cup like he might take a drink but never did. He set it back down and looked at me. "I was only seventeen when I found out his mother was pregnant. I had a football scholarship on the line and big plans. I couldn't see how a kid could mix into my future, so I gave up all rights. I told his mother that I wanted nothing to do with him."

"Why do you want to make things right now?"

"His mother died in a car crash four days ago, and I'm all he has left. He reached out to me, and I saw it as my chance to make things right."

I tucked my curls behind my ears. "Death is kind of a beautiful thing. It makes us view life in a new perspective, shows us what is really important, and opens our hearts to forgiveness. Even if it's forgiving ourselves."

"Yeah, I guess so." He finished off his coffee and tore his napkin in half. "Do you have a pen?"

"I do." I dug in the side of my bag until I found one. I handed it to him. "Here."

He wrote something down and slid it toward me. "Keep me updated on how your visit goes."

I stared at his number and smiled. I grabbed the other half of the napkin and wrote my number down. I slid it across to him with a smile. "And you let me know how meeting your son goes."

He folded it and placed it in his pocket. "It was really nice to meet you, Nora."

"You too, Sean."

"Maybe our paths will cross again."

I stood and smiled. "That would be nice."

He kissed my cheek. "Merry Christmas."

"Yeah. Merry Christmas to you, too."

K.R. SMITH
The Last Snowfall

"This is unacceptable!" Santa Claus bellowed. "There's a child's name on my list without a present written next to it!" He turned to his helper elf and said, "It was your job, Felix, to check for problems like this. Now we're at this girl's house and I have no gift for her."

"Oh, dear—I was meaning to talk to you about that. We received Jasmine's letter, but it didn't mention what she wanted. There was only a drawing of a snowflake."

"A snowflake?"

"Yes, Santa," a tiny voice replied.

"Who said that?"

"I did. I'm Jasmine. I didn't know how to spell snowflake."

"I see. By the way, shouldn't you be asleep?"

"I didn't want to miss you. I had to know if you could help me. I promised my mother that someday I would take her back to the snow she loves. She was born in the north. Her name is Sarah. We only moved here because I needed to see a special doctor."

"Taking your mother on a trip should be easy enough once you're older," Santa explained. "Or perhaps I can arrange something for next year."

Jasmine sighed. "That's the problem, Santa. I don't think I'll have a 'next' year."

Santa noticed the bottles of medicine near her bed. He exchanged a concerned glance with Felix.

"I thought if I couldn't go with my mother to the north, maybe I could bring the snow here—with your help."

"I wish there was something I could do, but I don't make the snow."

"Then who does, Santa?"

"Why, the Old Man of the North, Boreas. Most know him as Father Frost. That's his job, along with sending forth the cold winter winds."

"Oh." Jasmine's shoulders drooped. "So you can't help after all."

"You can still have a present if you'd like. I'm sure we can find something on the sleigh."

"I don't really want anything else. Thanks."

Santa turned to Felix and whispered, "This isn't working. I've promised to deliver a gift for every good child. Now what am I to do?"

"Perhaps Boreas could send a little snow her way. That shouldn't be too much to ask."

"I don't know," Santa said while stroking his beard. "He's a bit of a grump, though I suppose we could try. Pull Comet and Dasher from the team—they're the fastest. Have them take you to Boreas. Explain the situation and ask if he can help. And remember to address him respectfully. You'll need all the help you can get."

AFTER THE long trip back north, Felix found Boreas sitting alone in his icy castle. He explained the situation.

"What? Nick must be out of his mind! I can't make snow that far south, even in the winter."

"You're our only chance, Father Frost. You have to try."

"It's impossible."

"Are you sure?"

"How? I could huff and puff all day and never make snow in that desert."

"You might if you had help."

"Help?"

Felix shuffled his feet and avoided eye contact. "Yes—help."

Boreas's brow furrowed. "Just what are you suggesting?"

"Your daughter—in the south?"

"That insolent child! Never! And I asked that the name Khione never be spoken in my presence."

"I didn't, Father Frost. You did."

"Humph! That's irrelevant."

"I hear she's very good at making snow."

"Well, of course. She *is* my daughter, after all."

"Then it might work?"

Boreas rolled his eyes. "I suppose it's possible that it isn't impossible."

"Then you'll try?"

"Oh, all right. But only if you'll do the asking," he said, pointing an icy finger at Felix's nose. "And I doubt she'll agree."

COMET AND Dasher barely had time to rest before starting the trip to the South Pole. Felix, nearly exhausted himself, made his best effort to convince Khione to work with her father.

"Father comes begging for *my* help? I hardly think so. He's too controlling. He wants everything done *his* way."

"He made particular mention of your ability to make snow. And how you're very special."

"He said that?"

"Words to that effect," Felix said, crossing his fingers. "Please, Khione, for Jasmine. Help her keep the promise she made to her mother. Surely you can understand."

"Well—only to make certain Father doesn't disappoint another little girl."

"Wonderful!" Felix said with a smile. "I'll make the arrangements."

IN THE gray skies above the desert, Khione and Boreas approached each other. Neither offered a warm greeting.

"Father?"

"Yes, Khione?"

"I want you to know I'm only here to help Jasmine."

"As am I—and as a favor to Nick. I suggest we get on with it."

EARLY CHRISTMAS morning, Jasmine awoke, rubbed her eyes, and looked out the window. A few white flakes drifted to the ground.

"Mother! Come quickly!"

Sarah, fearing something wrong, came running down the steps. "What is it, Jasmine?"

"Look, Mother! It's snowing!"

"Snowing? How can that be?"

"I asked Santa to bring snow for you. Can we go outside? I've never seen real snow before."

"Only for a moment. You're very weak. I'll have to wrap you up warmly."

LOOKING DOWN at Jasmine's house, Boreas grumbled as he observed the meager results of their efforts.

"I know we've each done our best, Khione, but there's little to show for it."

"Perhaps we can give it one more try, Father—together."

Boreas looked at his daughter and gave her just the tiniest hint of a smile, then nodded. "All right, then—together—on three."

"THE SNOW is really swirling now, Jasmine. It's just like I remember!"

Sarah looked into Jasmine's face. Her eyes were closed, her heart still. It was Jasmine's first snowfall, and her last. Sarah held her all that much closer as the glistening flakes danced around them. Jasmine had kept her promise—as had Santa—and, from that day on, every snowflake reminded Sarah of that most special Christmas of all.

BETH AVERY
Jack Frost Stops by for a Chat

Jack Frost is sitting on the stoop when I come out in the morning.

"I killed your ferns," he says with a smirk and points to a clump of fronds outlined with delicate white crystals.

"You know those are perennial, right? You didn't kill them. They're just dormant now. Frankly, I think you improved their appearance," I say.

"I was hoping they were tropical," he says mournfully.

"We go through this every year, Jack. How can you be a manifestation of Nature if you can't even remember what the basic laws of Nature are? I don't grow things that can't survive your frost," I scold.

"Jenny Letham down the street usually swears at me when I frost her plants," Jack replies.

"That's because Jenny grows scented geraniums and always waits too long to bring them in. She's the garden nursery's best customer. I seriously don't understand why you don't spend more time mocking her instead of coming here every first frost and trying to get a rise out of me," I say with a sigh.

"She cries. It makes me feel bad...well, you make me feel bad too, but it's a different kind of bad. You just make me feel stupid. Jenny makes me feel mean." Jack fiddles with a leaf, slowly tracing its veins with a light coating of frost.

I think for a while before I answer him on this. Jenny is the one who is stupid, and Jack isn't being mean when he frosts plants that can't survive our climate. My plants need the cold period to live, which is just one reason why I'm not a fan of Jenny's efforts to defy the laws of our winters. Jenny's delusional anger at Jack for frosting her tropical plants is not something that I want Jack to pander to. At the same time, I like this side of Jack, and I'm inclined to encourage these signs of a conscience. I decide not to directly respond to his concerns about Jenny.

"I really like what you did to the pine," I eventually say. "Your work really stands out on the dark green needles and the pine cones on that branch there."

Jack looks up. "It is pretty good," he says with a real smile. "I spent extra time on those pine cones because I knew you would appreciate it."

"I do. I always love when you come back for the winter. You make the whole world look like it's wearing a beautiful ball gown." I grin at him.

"I could come earlier if you miss me," he says.

I know he's testing. "No, no, Jack. The best thing about you is that you always come for a visit at just the right time. You're so wise for that," I add.

"Hmm." Jack puts the finishing touches on the ironwork around my door. "I guess it's a good thing to only visit just when people are starting to miss you."

"Absolutely, Jack. Absolutely. This is why we are such good friends," I say.

"Yes, that's exactly so. By the way, I just frosted your coffee. Hope you like it that way," he says.

He flies off before I can reply.

LAURA JAMEZ
Naughty or Nice

Holding the letter in his hand, Nick couldn't believe what he was reading. He got letters all the time from children all around the world asking, pleading, begging—even demanding—he leave them the presents of their dreams. But this was a first. He read it again:

Dear Father Christmas,

I am writing to you as I am fed up receiving coal in my stocking year after year. Now I know that down here coal is important, and I am grateful that you don't forget me, but this Christmas I would like a new set of tools. I have worked really hard at being good this year. I've kept the firepits blazing away without being asked. Everyone has commented on how much easier it has been to do their jobs without worrying that the fires are going to go out. Also, I passed all my exams with flying colors. I even broke the record for the number of new souls gathered by a novice. Mummy was so proud.

Anyway, I hope this letter finds you well and the run up to Christmas isn't too stressful. I will leave out the standard offer of condemning a soul of your choice to the Pits of the Underworld. (Daddy has asked me to remind you that the previous year's offers are no longer valid.)

*Regards,
Horace, age 12*

It had to be a joke, didn't it? Some kid having a laugh. "Meredith!"

The tinkling of bells from her hat announced Meredith's arrival. "Yes, Nick? Another hot chocolate?"

"No thanks, love. I'd like you to read this, and let me know what you think."

Meredith took the letter. "Mmm, I'll send for Tatters, see if he remembers this boy from the naughty list, check where he stays. Has to be a hoax, some little devil playing a joke on old Santa. Says he's twelve. A little too old to be writing letters."

A flurry of bells, a sprinkle of caster sugar, and she was back with Tatters and a large steaming mug of hot chocolate. Handing it over, she patted his hand. "I've put extra sprinkles in this one, you're going to need it."

Tatters took a breath. For the past thirty ears, he'd been delivering coal to the naughty children. The ever-increasing population on earth had meant the delivery of presents and coal all in one night by one person was nigh on impossible.

"It's no joke, Nick. First kid down in the Pits of the Underworld. Fluke of nature, seemingly. He's always received coal, cause… Well, he's a demon, ain't he? Stands to reason he's a bad un."

Nick drained his chocolate in one gulp and placed it carefully on the table. His hands only showed a slight tremble that this news had shocked him. He picked up the letter again, the words having new meaning. "Well, this kid seems to think he's been good. Not his fault his parents are who they are, and look," he held up the letter, "see how polite he is, respectful almost."

Tatters and Meredith exchanged a look. They knew what was coming. Nick never could resist a well-penned letter.

"Let's get him his tools. Make his Christmas this once, though I think you should deliver it, Tatters. You know the area, and we're not sure how the reindeer would cope with the heat."

REBECCA FYFE
A Christmas Dance

Delia's thin frame presented an unusual grace as she pirouetted and spun outside the high-end clothing store. Colorful Christmas lights twinkled from the decorations the town council had commissioned from the town's holiday decorating budget.

Music played from an old CD player, which sat beside the plastic cup she'd set out for donations. She'd spent her last dollar buying some cheap batteries from the dollar store and desperately hoped they held out long enough for her to gain at least some coins to allow her to buy some warm food tonight.

The chill of the winter air only made Delia dance more fervently. The snow coating the ground reached icy fingers through her worn ballet slippers.

She elegantly maneuvered her dance steps. Born with a natural talent for dance, she'd trained as a child before the accident had taken her family. It had been five years since the day she lost everything and everyone she loved at the age of thirteen.

Despite the stunning choreography of the dance and the precision and passion in her movement, no one stopped; no one parted with any coins from their tightly clutched purses or wallets. People brushed by her, too busy shopping for last-minute gifts to even notice her as she performed in the freezing cold. Some who walked by her were eating rolls and pastries bought from local shops. Delia concentrated on her dancing and tried to ignore the enticing aroma of food and the cramping of her empty stomach.

Tomorrow was Christmas. These Christmas Eve shoppers had warm homes to get to and families to spend time with. Delia had only her dancing.

As night fell and snowflakes began to drift down once more, creating a fresh blanket of white on the ground, Delia gathered her meager possessions: one worn and holey sweater, her CD player, two music CDs and an empty plastic cup. She also had a pair of shoes, which she exchanged for the ballet slippers on her feet. She noticed the slightly bluish tint creeping over her numb toes.

Delia found a dry spot under the overpass from the road. Less snow had crept into the covered area. It was the driest place she could find for the night. This wasn't her first night sleeping in the short tunnel, and she knew that the walls would help block some of the cold wind.

She curled herself into a tight ball and tried to sleep despite the uncontrollable shivering of her limbs and the constant gnawing ache in her belly from lack of food.

Delia was almost asleep when a bright light filled the underpass, making her open her eyes. She couldn't see anything at first as the white light filled her vision, but the warmth that filled the underpass gave her immediate relief from the constant chill.

As her eyes adjusted to the light, a woman took shape in front of her. Delia didn't recognize her, but the kindness in the woman's eyes reminded her of the way her mom used to look at her.

The woman had soft, shoulder-length golden hair, wore a pristine white pantsuit and smiled at Delia. She reached her hand out to Delia, and Delia didn't hesitate to take it.

They rose up through the ceiling of the underpass, and Delia didn't question how they could be doing this as a feeling of overwhelming joy filled her heart. She was going home to be with her family again.

MARJIE MYERS
TO THE TOP OF THE TREE

On December 1st, the Hornby family gets together and makes Hornby senior's stark home look like someone threw up Liberace's wardrobe. It's a day he looks forward to.

On December 2nd, the carefully placed angel is always missing, turning up hidden in the branches or caught beneath the tree skirt. This year, he decided to place a star on top instead. Everyone wished him luck in keeping it there.

CHIPPY, THE wooden toy soldier, had stood beneath the branches of every tree that Mr. Hornby had. It was his job to make sure the baubles stayed sparkly and that the tinsel was hung evenly around the tree.

Chippy loved his job and when Mr. Hornby had left the angel, Mirabelle, in the box, his poor little wooden heart almost went up in flames. After marching over, he decided that Mirabelle belonged atop the tree.

He opened the box.

"Mirabelle, are you in there? The tree is decorated. Mirabelle…"

Mirabelle sprang out like a jack-in-the box with a look of sheer panic across her face.

"Mr. Hornby can't have finished. How can he have finished when I haven't been unrustled?"

"He said the star won't run away and hide like you."

"But, that's my place."

"Go up there, then."

"Up there? But i-it's so very high. And the ground is so very far from up there."

"Okay, then back in the box."

"But…but…I won't see Christmas. I won't see the lights twinkling in the evening or racing each other or doing fancy flash dances. I won't be able to listen to the flower fairies share their stories. Oh Chippy, why do I have to be so scared of falling?"

"Don't be. I will catch you! I believe that you can do anything. I know it in my grain. Why don't you try and see?"

"It's so high…"

"You have to trust me. I won't let you down. Take my hand, and I shall help you. You see, the first branch is the easiest." And he lifted her up. "The hard part is to keep going, when you doubt yourself, when you think you might go wrong, or when you have to trust someone else and, yet, you doubt them too. That's the hard part, Mirabelle."

Mirabelle reached up and pulled herself to the next branches. She felt spurred on to reach the next one, but she wasn't sure how to get there.

She looked down at Chippy and felt quite dizzy, then looked up at Glimmer sparkling in the night. She wanted to move on but didn't know how. Mirabelle felt like crying, but something floated down in front of her. It was Mr. Silver, the tinsel. He gave a rustle and reached out to her. She realized he was offering to help, and he pulled her up to the fourth branch.

All she needed was to have some faith and a little hope, and she could find a solution. Looking around, she wondered how she would climb the next two branches. She saw a bauble glistening in the light and had an idea. She would have to ask for help, something that didn't come easy to her.

"Excuse me, Orb. Could I swing on you up to the next branch? I am aiming for the top, but I can't get there alone. Will you help?"

"Yes. Would you help me also?"

Mirabelle was taken aback. No one ever asked her for help. Instead, they laughed at her and mocked her saying, "Whoever heard of an angel who fears heights?" They never thought she had much to offer.

"Of course, Orb. What shall I do for you?"

"On my top is a hoop with a soft silk ribbon running through it. Beside it, a sharp pine needle is sticking into me. It's terribly annoying putting up with a prickle like that all day."

Very carefully, Mirabelle removed the pine needle for Orb.

"Oh! That is much better. Now, climb aboard and let's get swinging."

As Mirabelle leaped, she realized she might not reach the branch, but she just made it. Hanging by her fingertips, she told herself not to look down. But she did. Instead of feeling scared, she felt very safe indeed. Standing at the bottom of the tree was Chippy, smiling and ready to catch her.

When she saw Orb still swinging, she caught her reflection in his coat of glass. The angel she saw didn't look scared. As her grip began to loosen, she closed her eyes expecting to freefall, and was surprised when something grabbed her and pulled her up to the top branch. When she opened her eyes, she saw it was Glimmer.

He had climbed down a little from his place on the tree to help her, even though he must have known why she was there. Her heart felt so full she thought she would burst.

For the first time, she took in the view from the top of the tree, and saw how beautiful it was. Mirabelle hadn't realized, she hadn't wanted to see it before. She looked down and blew a kiss to Chippy and then turned to Glimmer and gave him a smile. She had made it. She had overcome her fear with the help of her friends. They had believed in her, taught her not to be scared and given her hope, and here she was at the top of the tree to stay.

IT WAS December 2nd and Mr. Hornby came downstairs. He half expected not to see the star on the tree, but there it was. He smiled as he headed to the kitchen, stopping to remove his spectacles. He gave them a good clean, put them back on and looked at the tree again.

And there on the tree, sitting just below the star, was his angel.

TERRY CROUSE
ONE MAGICAL NIGHT

It began as a particle of dirt on the forest floor, lifted by an autumn storm into the upper echelons of the atmosphere. Currents and pockets of air made it dance and swirl amid clouds of particles and moisture, high above the earth. The dance continued until it collected enough ice and sank beneath the clouds as a magnificent snowflake. Slowly and gently, it drifted and swayed in the breeze in a gradual spiral down to earth before landing on the nose of a gray wolf.

The wolf sniffed the air as his nose began to tingle. The icy snowflake caused it to itch until he sneezed. Though he still felt its presence, he was distracted by the view overlooking the snow-covered village below. Bright colored lights illuminated the gabled roofs of homes and spires of churches. A chorus of voices sang words of cheer, notions of peace and hopes of good will—words and concepts the wolf could neither understand nor comprehend, yet he felt something stirring within himself he'd never felt before. Something besides hunger or fear or the instinct to survive. Even though he could smell prey nearby, he had little inclination to hunt, or even remain with his kind. He wandered away from the pack and headed down toward the village.

He made his approach with the greatest of caution. Villagers were accustomed to shooting wolves on sight, so he did not wish to draw any attention. Groups of carolers dotted the tree-lined streets, dressed in bright greens and reds and shivering in the wintry gales. Stealthily, he followed the scent of sheep toward the center of town, overwhelmed by the dazzling light displays and abundant decor along the way.

The town center hosted a large manger scene, populated with the standard Christmas icons such as Mary and Joseph and the baby Jesus. But what concerned the wolf most was the live display of animals, particularly the sheep. For a moment, his eyes dilated and his heart began to race wildly as his mind flew into images of hunting and death. But for a reason that he failed to understand, on this particular night, he had no inclination to hunt or kill. He merely tucked his head submissively and sauntered passively toward the nativity.

It was the strangest of scenes as the wolf came into full view of the small gathered crowd. The wolf wasn't howling, and the people weren't screaming. In fact, the people weren't moving much at all even though the wolf was within a few yards of them. The wolf walked on, bolder now, and with purpose. No one moved. Time stood still as fifty faces stared in awe as this lone gray wolf knelt alongside a sheep within the wooden manger, and the sheep never bleated or attempted to run. In fact, none of the donkeys or other sheep moved so much as a muscle. It was as though a gray wolf in the nativity was always meant to be.

Much of the crowd moved in for a closer look, taking pictures and marveling at the miracle before them. Predator and prey, side by side. A perfect poetic symbol for the season of giving and light. A little girl, hand-in-hand with her mother, walked up to the wolf and felt of his fur, dazzled by its softness. Curious, she felt his cold nose and wiped the snowflake off onto her finger.

"Look, Mommy! A snowflake!"

Her mother noticed the unique crystalline symmetry on the tip of her daughter's index finger, a large white flake of immaculate perfection. The little girl placed it on the end of her own nose and displayed it proudly and thanked the wolf for his gift. The wolf, for his part, was happy to oblige and be thanked by a human. He had never been the recipient of such gratitude.

The group continued to sing as they encircled the manger. "Silent Night" was soon followed by "God Rest Ye Merry, Gentlemen." The wolf didn't know the words, any words, so he did what wolves do, and howled. Mightily.

Aaaah-ooooooooooooooooh!

In the distance, over the hilltops, the other wolves responded in kind.

Aaaah-oooooooooh!

Howling in cadence with the carols, the hills and forests echoed the villagers.

Stars sparkling, moon glowing, snow drifting, chimneys puffing—all was right and perfect in the world, for this one blessed, magical night.

REBECKA VIGUS
WHAT IS THIS CHRISTMAS?

Winter in the fairy glen was not magical. The fragile fairies were forced to remain inside. Twit watched the snowflakes gently falling. She saw the brightly colored lights of the farmhouse across the meadow. She longed to see what the family was doing. Her wings twitched with the urge to fly. Maybe she would slip out tonight. What could it hurt? What a great adventure! Just then her mother called, "Lights out."

Twit curled into her bed. Moonlight streamed through the window as she lay down to sleep. She waited until all was quiet before easing out the window into the night.

The bitter cold wind made it hard for her to fly, but the moonlight through the clouds helped her keep her bearings. Those beautiful snowflakes were cold and wet as they hit her gossamer wings. She hoped she would make it to the farmhouse.

It seemed to take forever and just as she was about to give up, Twit smacked into a windowpane. She rubbed a spot with her cold hand to see inside. A little girl was lying on her bed reading. The room was all pink and cozy. Twit tapped on the window, hoping the girl would let her in. She was about to give up a when little boy ran into the room.

He shouted muffled words Twit could not make out. Then he noticed her. "Look, Bridget," he yelled. "There's a weird bug on your window."

Both children came to the window. Twit was excited, hoping they would let her in so she could get warm.

"It's a fairy," Bridget said.

"There's no such thing," the boy stated. But he continued to stare at the strange bug. It looked like it was waving to them.

"Stand back," Bridget ordered. "I'm going to open the window and let it in." She lifted the window enough to reach out and grab the little fairy. "Oh, she's cold."

Twit was startled by having her own wish come true and could only sit it Bridget's hand and shiver.

"Find me a doll blanket will you, Bryce?" Bridget asked.

He muttered but started searching through her doll stuff. "Will this work?" he asked, holding up a doll washcloth.

"Just bring it," Bridget ordered. "She's freezing." Bridget wrapped the tiny fairy to help her get warm. "Do you understand what I say?" she asked.

Twit nodded yes.

"I'm Bridget, and this is Bryce," she told the fairy. "Did you come for Christmas?"

Twit looked confused she answered, "I'm Twit. What is this Christmas?"

"You don't know what Christmas is!" Bryce shrieked.

"Hush, or Mom will hear us," admonished Bridget. "Christmas is a holiday we celebrate every year. We decorate the house, hang our stockings, and wait for Santa to arrive."

"What's a Santa?" Twit asked.

"This is messed up," Bryce said. "Everybody knows who Santa is. He lives at the North Pole. Every year he brings toys to girls and boys around the world. He rides in a flying sleigh pulled by reindeer."

It was Twit's turn to be astonished. She had seen Santa and his sleigh. She never knew what he did. She sneezed.

"Oh, we can't let you get sick," Bridget said. "I'll fix you a bed and tuck you in. Tomorrow we can talk more."

Twit perched on a pillow wrapped in the washcloth as Bridget went to work making her a bed. Once made, Bridget shooed Bryce from the room and tucked Twit into bed. She crawled into bed and shut off the light. "Night, Twit."

"Night."

Sometime in the night, Twit spiked a fever and got chills. She knew this was not good, and she would never make it home by morning. Her mother would worry. She tossed and turned in the little bed.

Bridget found Twit soaking wet and shivering in the morning. "Oh, you poor thing. Let me find something to make you better." She left the room, and Twit curled into the bed trying to get warm.

In a few minutes, Bridget returned with a tiny doll cup. "Drink this, it will help."

Twit drank while Bridget searched for dry bedding. She tucked the little fairy in. "I hope you get well soon. I made a Christmas wish to keep you."

Twit cried, "I made a wish to go home."

"Sleep now, and we can work it out when you feel better." Again, Bridget tucked Twit in and left the room.

When Twit woke up she felt better. She tried out her wings and flew to the window. Snow covered everything, and she could hardly see her home in the woods. She cried, wishing once again she was safe at home.

When Bridget came back, she had Bryce in tow. "We talked it over and decided we are going to help you get home."

Twit smiled. "Thank you."

"You need to drink some more of this because we have to take you outside," Bridget told her.

Twit took the cup and drank. She was surprised it did not make her sleepy. She handed the cup to Bridget.

"Bryce and I are going to get ready to go out," she said. "We'll be back to get you in a few minutes."

The two left the little fairy. She worried they might change their minds and keep her there forever. Tears stung her eyelids. They had been so kind. It took ages, but the two returned dressed in their snowsuits.

"Hop into my pocket," Bridget said, opening the pocket on her jacket. "Can you show us the way?"

"Oh, yes," Twit said, climbing in.

In less than ten minutes, they were across the field.

At the outskirts of the woods, Twit said, "I can get there from here. Thank you." She fluttered her wings and flew home.

Twit sent her wish to Santa and on Christmas morning Bridget found a fairy-sized doll in her stocking, and Bryce found the slingshot he wanted.

REBECCA FYFE
The Yuletide Exchange

Cassandra lit candles all over the house and opened her front door. Moonlight filtered in, spotlighting the holly and mistletoe hanging in decorative wreaths and garland around her home.

The Yule tree was in place. She had decorated it with ribbons and colorful baubles. The Yule log was in the fireplace, lit with the remnants of last year's log. She did one quick look around the house, checking that everything was ready for Yuletide celebrations. Once that was done, she looked out the front door again. It was almost time.

A large black dog walked up beside her and sat down. He was a massive dog. His black eyes shone with a faint reddish hue. For a hellhound, he wasn't a terrible companion, but he'd eaten enough to nearly push her into poverty this past year. He had an appetite to match his unusual size. He had also violently objected to any male within ten feet of Cassandra. She had a few female friends who he tolerated, but any of the men she had been friends with before this past year, her hellhound had scared away.

She'd had no choice but to take care of him. He'd been left in her care when the Wild Hunt passed during the previous Yule, when the

Hunt had taken her brother. She'd been obliged to take good care of this brute of a dog if she had any hope of getting her brother back during this year's Yuletide. She just needed to confront the Wild Hunt.

Cassandra glanced anxiously out the door again. It was her brother's fault he'd been taken. He didn't believe in celebrating Yule, and he mocked the idea of the hunt. She'd warned him that her home was in its path and not to go out that night, but he hadn't listened. The Wild Hunt must have caught up with him as he walked home from the pub.

The only evidence she'd had of what happened was this enormous hellhound she had found sitting on her doorstep the next morning. For lack of a better name, she'd taken to calling him "Beast." He was good company when he wasn't scaring people away, and he'd taken to sleeping across her legs at the end of the bed each night. A part of her didn't want to see the creature go, but she needed this hell-beast as an exchange for her brother when the Wild Hunt came back tonight.

A flock of crows flew past the windows, circling the house, their screeching caws grating on her ears. Cassandra felt goose bumps rise along her arms and a tingling at the back of her neck and knew it was time. She grabbed her coat and, slipping her arms into the sleeves, stepped out the door to greet Odin and the spirits of the dead who followed him on the hunt.

At first, she couldn't see anything through the fog that surrounded her, but she could hear dogs barking, the beat of hooves against the road and voices, though she couldn't make out what the voices were saying.

Gradually, shapes became clearer through the mist until the Wild Hunt drew to a stop before her. Cassandra looked up at the gray-haired, bearded man astride a magnificent black stallion. He was taller and more muscled than most men, and he wore all black.

"I invite you to partake of the food I have prepared to sustain you during the hunt," Cassandra said in a loud voice, sounding more assured than she felt.

Wispy shapes moved around Odin, and she could still hear many voices, all speaking at once, none loud enough to drown out Odin's voice as he accepted her offer. Several mounts behind him held men who were more substantial than the spirits of the dead who surrounded him, but she dared not look away to check if her brother was among them.

Odin signaled the men to enter her house. Three went inside and returned with the platters of food she'd set out on her table earlier. While the food was passed out to the huntsmen, Odin's gaze rested on the beast of a dog at her side.

"What do you think, Fenrir? Are you ready to come home now?" Odin addressed the hellhound.

Fenrir's response was a low growl, causing a deep, booming laugh to burst forth from Odin.

"It appears you have enchanted my dear friend, Fenrir," Odin said to Cassandra. "You have done well, and your brother will be returned to you by morning. I'm afraid you will have to keep Fenrir for longer though. He is refusing to leave your side."

Cassandra ignored the part about keeping the hellhound and focused on his words about her brother. She was getting him back! Excitement bubbled up inside her.

"I thank you, my lord. May you have a successful hunt this night." She gave a small curtsy.

Odin gave a smile and a wink as he signaled the hunt onward.

As they disappeared into the distance, Fenrir's shape began to distort and blur in front of her. Within moments, a thickly muscled, bare-chested man stood before Cassandra. He had black hair that reached to his shoulders in soft waves, bright green eyes and a strong chin. His gaze on her was tender.

"Fenrir?" Cassandra couldn't help the squeak that snuck into her voice.

"In the flesh," he said, a slightly wicked smile appearing.

She turned to lead him back into the house, glancing over her shoulder as she paused. "You're *not* sleeping in my bed tonight, Beast," she huffed. "You can sleep on the couch."

"As you wish." His smile never faltered as he followed her into the house.

Cassandra turned back to continue into the house, hiding her smile from him. This was going to be the best Yuletide yet. She was getting her brother back, and the year ahead looked full of promise.

TOM MOHAN
Scarred

Marci shivered as a breeze washed off the Pacific Ocean and onto the boardwalk. Gone were the summer scents of sunscreen and barbecue, replaced by odors of brine and seaweed. The faux gas lamps that lined the boardwalk were decked with aged wreaths and an occasional cottage radiated holiday cheer. The rest appeared abandoned for the winter.

Late afternoons in San Diego were often sunny this time of year, though this day a haze had settled over the coast. Marci looked around at the scattering of families and beach volleyball players beginning to pack up, ready to leave the day behind and return to the comfort of their homes. None of them seemed to feel the chill that flowed through her veins.

Marci's left hand pulled her jacket tighter around her throat while her right clutched tight the McDonald's bag. She couldn't stand McDonald's herself, but Max loved the stuff, and she owed it to him to give him what he liked.

"Hey, babe, this is the beach. Show some skin. You afraid of the sun or something?"

Marci ignored the stranger's comment and kept walking. No, she didn't fear the sun. She trembled at the stares that would follow her like a snarling hound. The comments she would endure. The scars she hid beneath her clothing were not for public viewing. They would never understand.

She caught sight of Max sitting in his usual spot on the weathered sea wall between the beach and the boardwalk. Even from this distance Marci could see the long wisps of what little hair he had left blowing in the breeze. She grasped the food bag tighter and swallowed the lump that never failed to form in her throat at the sight of her husband. As she drew nearer, the stains and rips in Max's old trench coat grew more pronounced. She had brought him fresh clothes on many occasions, but he would never take them, just as he would never come home.

Marci brushed the sand from the three-foot wall before climbing onto the spot beside him. Her left arm lightly touched his right. She found that she was growing accustomed to his smell. "How are you today, Max?" she asked.

He remained still, as though unaware of her presence. Maybe he was. She was never sure. He stared out into the depths of the sea, his clear, blue right eye alive with an internal fire.

"The hyenas have eaten the squirrels that the garbage men left behind," he said.

Marci felt the corners of her lips turning up in a small smile. "Hyenas, huh?"

Max shifted toward her, and her smile faded as the ruined left side of his face came into view. "Hyenas with mohawks. Purple ones," he said.

"Purple mohawks or purple hyenas?" she asked, but the sea already drew his attention. Once again, she could only see the rugged, beautiful side of his face.

"I brought you some burgers," Marci said as she placed the bag in his lap. He sat, staring, not acknowledging the gift. "Please, Max.

Please come home with me." The words were out before she could stop them. Max remained silent, but his right hand moved to rest on her knee. As always, his touch took her back to the accident. Back to the sound of her own screams as Max struggled to free her from the wreckage. Back to the sight of her husband engulfed in flames. Back to her own agony that left her with few other memories of that night. Now she hid beneath layers of clothing while he hid somewhere deep within his own mind—a place of purple, mohawked hyenas. A place she could never go.

Marci shivered again. Max gave her knee a light squeeze before lifting his hand from her leg. He held it out at arm's length; fingers open wide so he peered through them.

"The moon danced with the stars, and they had a baby," he said.

Marci sighed. "I'm so cold. So cold inside."

"A baby squirrel," Max said as he closed each of his fingers until only his index finger remained extended.

Marci watched as he raised the finger until it rested just below the hazy form of the sun. He held it there until she was certain his finger glowed. Finally, he turned toward her, the look on his face never changing. He brought the tip of his glowing finger to the tip of her nose, like a parent might do to a child. Marci felt a relaxing warmth spread through her face, then down her entire body. She closed her eyes, relishing the first warmth she had felt in a long time. After only a few seconds his touch moved away, yet the warmth remained in her heart.

Content for the moment, Marci rested her head against her husband's shoulder. "Merry Christmas, Max."

Max only grunted as he stared out at the ocean, but it was enough. For today, it was enough.

GLEN DAMIEN CAMPBELL
The Gift

Something was amiss, Joe Clarke was sure of it. His sister, Sally, who was typically a rather easy-going character, was being suspiciously insistent about things.

It had started that afternoon after she showed up at his place to insist that they drive back to Folkestone together so Joe could spend Christmas with her, "boring" Barry and the brats, even though two weeks earlier he had turned down that invitation without any objection. Maybe the thought of her lonely, loser brother spending Christmas alone had run amuck on her conscience.

After finally getting Joe to accompany her, she drove only halfway to Folkestone before steering the car into a hotel parking lot, insisting on getting a room for the night.

"It's too dangerous to drive on these icy roads at night," she argued.

After they had checked into adjoining rooms, Sally spilled soda on Joe's shirt and insisted he change into his Cannibal Corpse t-shirt—the very same t-shirt she had insisted he bring along.

"Why do you want me to wear this?"

"Because, I bought you two tickets for Christmas to go see them," Sally explained. But something seemed off. Pushy wasn't Sally's nature, yet now she was even insisting on him going out to the side street kiosk to buy cigarettes.

"I thought you quit!"

"I did," she said. "But it's Christmas, I'm allowed to indulge."

"Okay, but if I go get 'em, you pay for the pizza I order when I get back, deal?"

"Fine," Sally agreed.

Joe took the money she held out and then began buttoning up his coat.

"Don't do it up!" Sally barked.

"Why not, it's cold out there?"

"Don't be a wimp. You're not going far, and buttoning up makes you look fat."

He scowled at her.

"If you think saying that is gonna make me not want pizza you're wrong."

JOE WAS gone.

On his way to meet his destiny, Sally thought, knowing she was being overly dramatic. But, heck, why not? It had taken a lot of effort on her part to get to this moment.

Wasting no time, she raced over to the light switch, turned off the lights and then darted over to the window, which looked out onto the street. Pulling back the curtains slightly, she peeked out the window and, after a moment, saw Joe emerge from the hotel—his awkward, skulking gait unmistakable. As he trudged through the snow, she watched him count the money she had given him, probably trying to figure out how much change he could siphon off without her noticing.

Jeez, when will he grow up?

He was still counting the money when he arrived at the kiosk, which was being manned by a dark-haired woman swaddled in a brown anorak with a fur-lined hood, looking every bit like an Eskimo except for the nose stud, black nail polish and heavy mascara. Her name was Nikki, and Nikki, not the inclement weather, was the real reason Sally had wanted a night's stop over at a two-star hotel.

When Joe had first turned down the invitation to spend Christmas with her, Barry and the kids, Sally was relieved. There'd be no awkward forced conversation between Barry and Joe, and no death metal instead of Christmas carols. Christmas had suddenly become a lot easier, if maybe a little duller.

But then Sally met Nikki.

It was after another "it will never happen again" rendezvous with Frank from IT. Sally needed a smoke and some fresh air. The hotel room she was staying in reeked of sex and betrayal, so she left for the kiosk, where she was served by Nikki, who was wearing a Cannibal Corpse t-shirt.

"That's my brother's favorite band," Sally commented casually, but that was all it took to set Nikki off.

Twenty minutes later, Sally walked away from the kiosk with more information about Nikki than she knew what to do with. Garrulous, metal-obsessed, and attracted to slackers, Sally wanted to tie a ribbon around her; she was perfect for Joe.

"I should have planted a bug on him," Sally said nervously, watching Joe speak to Nikki for the first time.

She watched as Nikki turned around and plucked a pack of Marlboros off the tobacco shelf.

"C'mon!" said Sally impatiently.

Nikki turned back around and handed the cigarettes to Joe, pointing at his t-shirt.

"That's right," muttered Sally. She smiled broadly, feeling pleased with herself. "You both have the same lame taste in music. Why don't ya talk about it?"

Sally relaxed. The t-shirt had worked. They were talking. Success! She had brought the two metal-head singletons together and provided a conversation starter to help them get acquainted. Now it was time for Joe's wit and charm to takeover.

You're a better person than you think you are, Joe. You can do this!

For ten minutes she watched them talk. Nikki was leading the conversation, but a line was forming behind Joe. He needed to wrap things up.

"Tell her about the concert tickets!" Sally screeched, and then, almost as if he had heard her, she saw Joe raise two fingers. "Very good, Joe. You have *two* tickets for that shitty band you both like. Now, ask for her number!"

She saw Nikki pick up a scrap of paper and start to scrawl onto it. When she was done, she handed it over to Joe.

Sally cheered triumphantly.

"WHAT ARE you smiling about?" Sally asked when Joe returned to their hotel room wearing a dopey grin.

"I got a number," he said.

"Oh, yeah?"

"Yeah, the woman working the kiosk gave it to me." He held up the scrap of paper Nikki had given him. "She says it's the best pizza place in town, and it's two for one!"

ERIC SPROLES
Christmas 1916

It was dark now, the night of December 24th, 1916, the sky occasionally lit up by artillery and machine gun fire. Edward had only been on the Western Front for just a little over two months. Before enlisting with half of his class, he had been in his third year studying at Cambridge University.

Of course he, as well as many other students, enlisted out of a sense of pride and to serve his country in the Great War. He had never regretted or doubted his decision, although it saddened him that he had lost so many friends and even fellow classmates during the fighting.

Even now, as he leaned back against the trench wall, he could still hear the artillery and machine gunfire rage on. For most of the day, the fighting along the trenches had been intense.

He lit a cigarette and took a long draw upon it, briefly forgetting where he was. Carefully he reached into the breast pocket of his uniform and took out the gold locket he kept with him always.

He slowly opened the locket and gazed at his love, the beautiful Victoria. They had met the year before at the university and began dating shortly after. He took another draw on the cigarette as he closed the locket and held it close to his heart.

It was then that he noticed the silence. No longer could he hear machine guns or artillery. Instead, he heard the faint sound of what appeared to be singing.

He strained to hear. Yes, there it was. It seemed to be coming from not only his trench, but also in the distance from the enemy trench as well. It was the sound of songs of Christmas and the holidays.

Edward could not believe what he heard: the sweet music of home and warmth. He looked up as he felt the first snowflakes coming down, touching his skin.

It was at this moment, more than any other, that he realized everything would be okay. Even though he was far from his home and the woman loved, he was not alone.

He knew without a doubt that he would be all right, and he'd return home safe and sound once again to see his dear Victoria.

For the rest of that night and on Christmas Day, there was only the sound of songs being sung.

J.S. BAILEY
Scratch

The child, Devon, lay shivering in his bed on Christmas Eve—not because it was cold, but because something lurked in his room that shouldn't have been there.

He could feel it trying to creep into his heart, though he couldn't see it. In fact, the only reason he knew it was there at all was because of the soft scratching sound it made within the walls, like something trapped trying to get out.

And it wasn't the first he'd heard it. Just last week as Devon sat on his bedroom rug transforming his extensive Lego collection into an armada of alien ships, he'd heard a sudden scratching near his bed.

It had stirred something in his mind—an old memory, perhaps?—but whatever it was remained hidden.

"Oh, Devon, it's nothing," his mother had said when she came to investigate the sound, though of course by that time everything had fallen silent. "Probably just a neighbor playing around."

Devon supposed she might be right. He and his mother lived in a townhouse sandwiched smack-dab between two others, and sometimes the neighbors on either side got too loud and his mother would curse and bang on the wall to shut them up.

They'd never scratched around, though. Why would they, anyway?

Tonight, his mother had to pull an all-night shift at the hospital, so Devon's teenage cousin Georgia had been called in to babysit.

As the scratching continued frantically inside the wall by his head, Devon worked up the courage to call out. "Georgia?"

No answer.

"Georgia, come here!"

The scratching intensified. Devon could picture sharp claws grinding away at the inside of the wall, ready to poke through any moment. Unable to stand it any longer, he pulled himself from bed, wrapped his blanket around himself for extra protection, and raced out of his room and down the stairs.

Georgia, who'd dyed her hair black and always wore black clothes bedecked with silver studs and chains, was sitting on the living room floor by the Christmas tree sticking tape on a package she'd apparently just wrapped. She pulled a set of earbuds out of her ears and said, "Ho ho ho."

Devon just stared at her.

She set the tape and package aside and brushed her hands together. "Don't look so surprised."

"Georgia, there's…there's something in my wall."

A short bark of laughter escaped his cousin's lips. "Probably wires and insulation. Spoooooky."

Tears brimmed in Devon's eyes, and Georgia's expression softened. "You really think something's in there?"

Devon nodded and pulled the blanket tighter around him.

With a sigh, Georgia stood. Tonight she wore a short black skirt and black and white striped leggings that reminded Devon of witches—maybe she could cast a spell and make the scratching go away. "Fine, I'll check it out. If something tries to eat me, I'll kick its ass."

They started up the stairs together. Devon reached for Georgia's hand, and to his surprise, she took it and gave it a squeeze. "You okay?"

"No."

"Don't worry, bud. Hopefully it's just reindeer and elves."

They arrived in Devon's bedroom, and Georgia flicked on the light. She tilted her head and listened. "I don't hear anything."

As terrified as Devon had been, he prayed for the sound to come back so Georgia wouldn't think he'd been lying.

Georgia spoke again. "Are you sure you—"

Something started scratching the floor underneath the nightstand, and Georgia jumped. Staring transfixed at the source of the noise, she got down on her hands and knees and peered underneath it.

"That's weird," she said. "It must be under the floor now. Maybe we can—"

Whatever else she'd been about to say, Devon would never know, for Georgia had totally and completely disappeared.

"IT BUGS me that that girl just left you all alone last night," Devon's mother said the next morning as he tore into his presents. "Anything could have happened to you." She looked at the clock hanging over the mantel, her eyes bleary from the late shift. "I'll call her after breakfast and give her a piece of my mind."

Devon made no reply. He knew what he'd seen, and his mother would never believe him if he told her the truth.

He peeled the paper off a box that turned out to contain a remote-control Corvette. As he made what he felt was a convincing display of thanks and gratitude, the same scratching sound from before issued from somewhere up above.

Most likely his bedroom.

Devon's mother lifted her gaze toward the ceiling. "What in the world is *that*?"

"Mom, I—I told you something was up there. Remember the other day?"

Her tired eyes somehow looked even more exhausted than before. "It's just going to be a mouse, but if you want, we can go up together and check it out."

At once the image of Georgia disappearing arose in his mind, exposing another, deeper memory—the one he'd failed to remember before.

IT HAD been Christmastime then, too, though Devon had only the tiniest understanding of what that meant. Christmas was red and green and about baby Jesus and paper snowflakes and an old man who would bring you things, but only if you brushed your teeth and didn't talk back.

Devon had been poring through picture books in his room, and his father had been down in the kitchen whistling "Jingle Bells" and making cookies when something began to scratch around in the corner beneath his bed.

A picture book slid from his lap, forgotten, as the scratching quickened.

"Daddy?"

Below him, the whistling stopped. "What is it, Dev?"

Devon leaned over and peered into the shadows under the bed, seeing nothing move. "Something's under my bed."

"Hang on, I'll be up in a minute. No monster is going to stand a chance against me!"

Devon giggled, but his heart thumped harder. The longer he stared at the shadows, the more they seemed to take form, but what would they become?

He clamped his eyes shut before he could find out.

Then Daddy arrived in the bedroom doorway wearing a silly reindeer antler hat with jingle bells sewed onto it. "Now, let's see what's under there," he said with a smile.

Devon had always loved being around Daddy, who was tall and strong and made him feel safe. If there was one person in the world who could chase all the monsters away, it was Daddy.

Daddy paused and listened. "Hmm. Sounds like we've got a big, nasty mouse on our hands." He got down on all fours beside the bed and moved a box or two out of the way, and then Daddy, the man who made Devon and Mommy safe, disappeared.

DEVON REALIZED that his mother was staring at him. "Well?" she asked. "Do you want me to go up there or not?"

"No," he said. "You're right. It's probably just a mouse."

RAYMOND HENRI
The Giving Gift

For days, the anticipation of Christmas morning burned inside the pit of Wendell's stomach brighter than a hundred eternal Yule logs. He couldn't be bothered to run a brush through the mess of sandy hair curling every which way atop his head. He rubbed grit out of his green eyes to clear up the view of the stacks of presents forming a barrier around the ballroom's tree. His cheeks bore wrinkles from a still-warm pillowcase half a house away. The wrapped packages were so numerous that the colors and shapes were no less distinguishable once in focus than before. He had indeed received what any boy who had everything could want: more.

One particular parcel caught his attention more than the others. A thin, velvety blue box, square as it could be, hung from a tree branch amidst a halo of little white lights. No ribbon. No bow. Just his initials monogrammed in gold on the face of it. Tiptoeing, he made his way through the other packages to get a closer look. With care, he slipped the gift away from the tree and held it aloft, watching the lights catch on the monogram.

"Well, go on," his father's voice urged from behind. "Open it up."

Wendell looked back around to see his parents, robed and in an embrace. "What is it, Mom? Dad?"

"Bring it here, Wendell," his mother instructed as she bent down on her knees.

Wendell moved quickly through the field of presents as a delighted grin overtook his face. His father beamed and warmed his hands up in the pockets of his robe. Holding the lovely mystery box with both hands, Wendell skipped over to his mother.

"Now, Wendell," his mother began. "This box contains a one-of-a-kind treasure. Something so rare, your father and I had it specially made for you in Tibet by a magician."

Wendell's eyes grew wide. What rare treasure indeed could have come from such exotic origin? Certainly, such a thing that would drive his friends mad with envy. Could they even get one for themselves after learning of its existence? Didn't sound like it. Wendell slowly opened the box with awe and respect.

Attached to a thin silver chain, he found a round piece of gray metal that looked like a coin, etched with interesting symbols and designs he couldn't recognize. He freed the necklace from its velvety box and dangled it in front of his own puzzled face. More curious than excited now, he tried to decipher anything from the markings.

"This talisman," his father explained, "was made with the ability to empower its wearer with satisfaction. Your name and birthday have been specifically worked into the symbols to give it more strength and make it work for you alone."

"Do you like it?" his mother asked, arching her brow.

Wendell wasn't sure. It wasn't at all what he was expecting, but admittedly, it was one thing he didn't have. A magical amulet! It may not be the magic he would have chose, but it still sounded cool.

"I guess so," Wendell said, and then immediately became afraid that he sounded ungrateful. "Definitely, yes," he corrected. "May I put it on?"

His mother unclasped the necklace and helped situate the talisman around Wendell's neck. He didn't know what to expect. His parents held their breath and he was concerned that they, too, didn't know what might happen. There wasn't any sound, or light, or magical floating sensation. He wasn't sure he felt any different than before.

"Am I supposed to feel magicked?" he asked his parents.

They exchanged an amused glance, shrugging.

"We don't know," his father admitted. "The only instructions were to put it on."

"It looks nice, anyway," his mother offered. "Let's see what's inside these other presents, shall we?"

The three of them pivoted toward the forest of wrapping paper before them. Only this time, that burning sense of anticipation Wendell had felt before was gone. The warmth he felt now was more like a bath or his bed. He could barely muster up the curiosity to figure out what might be inside all those boxes. In fact, the mere act of opening them up seemed like a hassle and mess. And for what? Minutes of fascination until the gift felt less like a gift and more like something waiting to be replaced?

"What's wrong?" Wendell's mother asked, sensing his halting approach to the stockpile.

"I dunno. Maybe…" The thought got stuck in Wendell's mind. He couldn't think beyond the lack of wanting to open the presents. "Maybe, we could just take these to some kids who would want them."

MONA BLISS
WHAT'S GOOD FOR THE GOOSE

Ruthie skidded to a stop by my table saying, "Mike, she's at it again. You gotta get her out of the bar. Everyone is about to start taking their clothes off. You know how I feel about that hippie shit."

Ruthie is the bartender at the Hi-Brow, which is just down the block from the Denny's where I keep my office hours. She's not easily spooked and doesn't usually need help no matter who walks into her bar…except for one person who only shows up in L.A. on Christmas Eve. I grabbed my coat and threw some bills on the table.

"Jilly, I'll be back later." Jilly, pouring coffee for a customer, waved to me as we ran out the door and down Hollywood Boulevard to the dingy black bar with the neon sign of a martini glass tipping over onto the street.

Ruthie stopped at the door and looked at me. "I'm not going back in there, Mike. Not until you get her under control."

I sighed and pushed through the heavy door into a bar full of mellow Grateful Dead mayhem. Everyone was in varying states of undress and hugging and kissing on each other. Some seriously dirty dancing was happening out on the dance floor.

I finally spotted her sitting in the booth in the back, watching the room with a delighted smile on her jolly face. I stalked through the crowd, pushing people away as they tried to pull me into their stoned euphoria, straight to her table. She looked up at me innocently.

Loretta Claus is a handsome, plump woman of later years with beautifully styled snowy white hair, rosy cheeks, sparkling blue eyes and strangely modern glasses perched on her adorable little nose. Tonight, she was dressed in a stunning red suit with a plunging neckline and matching three-inch peep-toed heels.

"Mike! How lovely to see you. Won't you join me for a drink? We're having such a lovely time here tonight." She held out her hand to me as her eyes twinkled.

I tried to glare at her, but it's hard to do when someone smells like baking cookies and candy canes. "Loretta, I told you the last time you did this that if I caught you doing it again I was gonna tell Kris."

"Oh, pish posh! Kris is busy circling the world bringing joy to all the kiddies. If he'd come straight home when he was done, I wouldn't be here. We both know he's in Australia laying on a beach drinking beer. Am I supposed to stay in that frozen wasteland while he's on a *beach?* Screw that!"

She threw back what was left of her drink and looked over at the bar, noticing it was missing Ruthie. She eyed me suspiciously. "Ruthie went and got you, didn't she? Where is that girl? I swear this time I'm gonna put her on the Naughty List for sure."

I leaned down, putting both hands on the table in front of her and got nose-to-nose with her. "Lo, if you want another drink, you better knock this crap off right now. This place stinks of cinnamon, butter and caramel pheromones. These people are all high on supernatural sugar, and you're about to get 86'ed out of the last bar in L.A. that doesn't slam the door when they see you walk up."

She pouted and tried to make an excuse. Instead, I pushed in closer and softly said, "You know it's worse if I have to do it for you, Loretta. Just turn it off."

She snapped her fingers and suddenly the air in the bar cleared. No cookies. No candy canes. People slowly came back to their senses. Many rushed out of the bar although more simply carried on with what they were doing.

I stood up. "Now, if you behave, I'll buy you a drink, and we can catch up the way old friends do." She tried to be mad, but the promise of another Appletini won out.

Ruthie finally came back in. She headed straight to the register and began to prepare to close the place down.

I headed over to her. "Hold on, Ruthie. It's over now. I know it's hard to have much sympathy for her, but she doesn't have anywhere else to go tonight, and no one to be with. How about we cut her a little slack? You keep the bar open, and I'll stick around until it's time to send her home."

Ruthie closed her eyes and took a deep breath. "Mike, you owe me for this, buddy." She reached under the bar, pulled out a bottle of champagne, popped the cork and yelled, "Merry Christmas champagne for everyone on the house!"

Everyone cheered, and she poured two glasses, handing them to me. I turned and smiled at the plump lady standing next to me, beaming and fluttering her sparkling blue eyes my way.

LISA SHAMBROOK
The Little Mouse

Food was scarce, and the little mouse scampered hurriedly across the straw, avoiding hooves and scavenging poultry. A chicken screeched in his ear and he skidded aside, ducking quickly beneath the manger's wooden leg. He dragged a fresh piece of barley caught between his teeth and a couple of lost grains filled his swollen cheeks.

He peered out from behind the manger. Chaos had broken out over the last few weeks, and finding food had become a chore. His home was overrun with creatures of all kinds, and his daily route for food was constantly obstructed.

His bright black eyes stared with disbelief as yet more shouting rang out as another crude shelter was erected outside the livestock caves. A rough-hewn branch crashed down, its hollow thud resounding through the bedlam as it bounced and rolled. More yells and hasty footsteps followed before the makeshift roof was assembled, roped together above the temporary pens. He watched as more sheep and goats were crammed into the pens, and chickens flapped their irritated wings throwing dust into his eyes. He retreated into the pungent, dank straw, longing for peace and quiet.

The little mouse awoke from his nap as light began to fade and streaks of red filled the sky. He noted with relief that the busy footfall had diminished, moving into the streets rather than the livestock stalls. Music and chat poured from the buildings, and the sounds and the spices of evening meals curled up into the sky, along with spirals of smoke and fire, but it was quiet in his little neighborhood. The chickens slept, roosting upon beams and clustered in corners, the sheep cried out every now and then, and the goats had fallen silent. The donkeys in the stalls brayed softly, but these were familiar noises, and the little mouse was calm.

As darkness fell, the little mouse scurried to and fro collecting food and grains, and preparing for night.

His tranquillity was rudely interrupted by footsteps, tired voices and the weary drag of hooves on the dusty ground outside, and he scuttled back to his hole.

He squinted in annoyance as a donkey clumsily stepped into the cave and a woman slipped off, steadied by the man at her side. Another man dropped the donkey's rope, spoke quickly, and handed them an oil lamp before disappearing, leaving the couple alone in the dark stable. The lamp flickered, throwing dancing beams across the shadows and the man helped his wife settle into the straw. He dropped down beside her and wiped away the dust-stained tear that rolled down her cheek. A sheep bleated as a chill breeze wafted in, and the man took his weeping wife with her swollen belly into his arms. Her soft moans echoed, and the mouse withdrew.

It was very dark when the mouse woke again, and moonlight tried to gain entry through the front of the cave. The little mouse ventured out, scampering across the floor, but was stopped by the sudden cry that echoed in the gloom. He lifted his head and rose onto his hind legs, and stared into the shadows. The cry wasn't a lamb's mewling call, or the soft bray of a donkey, or even a goat's bleat, and the chickens were quiet… it was an unfamiliar cry, and he stared harder.

Lit only by glimmering lamp light, the corner threw oddly shaped shadows as the couple quickly wrapped a parcel in their arms. The mouse crept closer, every fiber of his tiny being both fascinated and fearful of the soft cries that emanated through the night. At the foot of the couple, the mouse stopped and gazed, and as he beheld, so did every other animal in the cave.

The young mother wiped tears from her face with her threadbare sleeve and kissed her newborn, and the little mouse climbed up onto the man's scruffy leather sandal. The little mouse could not take his eyes off the tiny babe and leaned closer. The man felt the scratch of tiny claws on his raw, weary feet and glanced down. He moved his hand and the mouse flinched, but the man took the mouse in his large, rough hand and brought him up, cradling the tiny creature against his chest. His heart thudded and he whispered softly, "And his name shall be Jesus, and you, little mouse, shall be the first to see him…"

The little mouse relaxed and peeped over the man's fingers, gazing in fascination and curiosity.

The noise from the late-night streets had subsided, and from the fields round about came an altogether different refrain. His large ears heard music vibrating in the air, strains of glory and joy, and shivers reverberated through the little mouse.

A glinting moonbeam sought out the child in its mother's arms and cast a halo around the babe, and the little mouse remained serene as the new dawn arrived…

MARISSA AMES
Thomas's New Coat

Thomas shivered in the sooty slush outside the workhouse. The February wind whipped sleet into his face. He wrapped his tattered coat about him, which had become too small in his year detained in the boys' ward.

Thomas lived in the best of times and the worst of times. In the age of wisdom and foolishness. The rich lived in three-story brick houses. The poor lived in workhouses.

The door opened, and his mother appeared. Emma wore her own dress. Gone was the striped inmates' uniform.

With teary eyes, Thomas slid on the slush and collided with his mother. She wrapped her arms around him.

"Can we stay away this time?" he begged. "Please?"

Thrice, Emma had discharged herself when she could be apart from Thomas no longer. Women lived separate from the men, and everyone separate from the children. Those three times, Emma left in her own dress, took Thomas to a park then returned by midnight. The workhouse promised food and shelter in return for hard labor. The streets promised starvation.

"Mama," he said, peering through his tears. "Please, Mama?"

With hands roughened by picking apart oakum, Emma combed through Thomas's hair.

"I'll pull carts in the mines," Thomas said. "I can still be a chimney sweep. I haven't grown much, really."

Closing her eyes in her gaunt face, Emma nodded.

As a widowed seamstress, Emma had managed to feed Thomas. Slipping in the slush during pea soup fog, she had injured her arm. She could not pay rent. After nights weeping in decision, Emma took Thomas to the workhouse.

Thomas had a plan. First, he would work as an errand boy. Then he'd be crossing sweeper, cleaning streets in front of rich ladies in exchange for tips. He would purchase matches to sell to passing shoppers. Thomas would enter the mines if he had no other choice. But, for his mother, he would work anywhere.

Offering domestic services in trade, Emma found a room in a London slum. Thomas worked as planned, waking before dawn and coming home late, with money for soup and suet.

As he worked, he advertised his mother's skills as a seamstress.

The owner of a new factory bought his matches. He had a job for Thomas's mother with the new sewing machines. Emma had only sewn with thread and needle, but she soon learned the machines, pushing the treadle with her foot. Only once did she sew over her own hand. Thomas worked within the same factory, carrying bolts of fabric. They worked twelve hours a day and returned together to their tiny room.

Thomas fell asleep fast. At night, his mother stitched by the single flickering flame of her lamp. Customers wanted coats with detail that only skilled seamstresses could provide.

One year after leaving the workhouse, Thomas wore the same tattered coat. Emma had purchased scraps of fabric from her employer. She had unpicked the seams of Thomas's coat and added the fabric to expand the sleeves. He had decent shoes, replaced when the others disintegrated. The slush did not invade the leather.

Luxury stopped at new shoes. Emma was ill. On good days, she worked at the factory, coughing into a handkerchief to catch the blood. On bad days, she sweated in bed with a fever. Half of November, Emma had worked at the factory. Twenty-four days into December, she had not worked at all.

Thomas trekked to the factory daily, buying food on the way home. After work, he cleaned the tenement to pay rent. Each night, Emma apologized as she fumbled with needle and thread while propped up in bed.

Thomas told her it didn't matter.

Emma fretted over Christmas. Last year, they resided in the workhouse. She couldn't see him at Christmas. This year, she had promised a hot meal with meat. Goose and figgy pudding, she said. She had promised it before she fell ill.

Emma had one match left. She used that last match to light a fire on Christmas morning, as snow fell in the streets.

Thomas held his only gift, complimenting how well Emma had wrapped it in old blankets. Warm from the fire, he unpicked the twine. Emma smiled weakly as he withdrew his new coat: thick, warm, and sturdy.

He slid his arms into the coat and hugged it around his body as his mother coughed blood into her handkerchief.

As Emma napped at midday, Thomas traversed the new slush of the London streets. What he sought lay ten streets away where Thomas had worked before finding the factory. Now other boys worked there, sloshing in sooty slush and broken shoes.

"Do you have matches?" he asked.

A boy half his age looked up with sunken eyes. Nodding and shivering, he said, "You have to pay for them."

A rag was wrapped around the boy's head, in lieu of a hat. His patched shirt hugged his body tightly. The boy wore no coat.

"I need them for my mother," Thomas claimed. "She's terribly ill."

Shaking his head, the boy said with chattering teeth, "My father will beat me."

Thomas needed those matches. He needed them for his mother, who kept him out of an orphanage simply by staying alive. Emma had taught him that he was better than no man, and no worse either. She taught him compassion and charity.

"Will you trade?" Thomas unbuttoned his coat. The boy's eyes lit up.

As the boy donned the coat and rolled the sleeves up, Thomas took his matches and sprinted home, sliding in the slush.

His own teeth chattered as he opened the door. He found his old, tattered coat. Emma woke as a log dropped from his frozen fingers onto the floor.

"Where is your new coat?" she asked.

Thomas added the log to the fire. Then he took her frail hands in his and told her of the little match boy. Someone needed the coat, just as Emma needed the matches.

"I'm sorry, Mama," he said, hoping for forgiveness. "I know you worked many nights on that coat."

Tears filled Emma's eyes. She spread her arms. As she embraced her son and his tattered coat, she whispered, "I worked harder to make you a good boy. You've given me the best Christmas present by proving you are one."

AILSA ABRAHAM
Unexpected Encounter

OXFORD STREET, LONDON, DECEMBER 18TH

They always got together to see the world-famous Christmas lights in town. It was an excuse to forget that they were in their 50s and old enough to know better. They bought sweeties and ate them walking along, necks craned upward, and the woman pointing and squeaking like a little girl. The man gave her indulgent smiles and hugged her close to his side. Wrapped in her warm coat with hand knitted woolly hat pulled down nearly to her eyes and matching scarf hiding all but her chin, she turned her face up to smile at him, radiant in the cold.

They were so enthralled with the lights above their heads that she didn't look where she was going and tripped over the legs of the old man, sprawled against the shop window.

"Oh, I'm so sorry!" She hunkered down immediately to make sure he was all right. "I wasn't looking. Are you okay?"

"No damage done, lady. Own fault. Should never have sat down to rest. I find I may not get up again," the old man mumbled into his beard. He was dressed shabbily but didn't smell of booze and was clean. Glancing up at her partner, there was a plea in her eyes. It was obvious he was used to this sort of thing as he also crouched down and spoke gently to the elderly gent on the pavement.

"I'm sure you must be getting cold down there. Shall we try to help you up?"

"Thankee, sir. That would be most gracious of you." The old man had a strange way of speaking as if he'd learned English from a very old language book. "I should be most obliged to you."

The man and woman helped him to his feet, holding his arms to steady him for a moment or two.

"Please, let us buy you a coffee or something. Have you been sat there for long? You must be freezing." The woman was all concern.

"That would also be most congenial of you, lady. I should prefer a large mug of cocoa if that were possible…and perhaps a mince pie?"

Bursting out laughing they agreed. It was, after all, nearly Christmas as they led him across the road to the nearest café.

"Were you Christmas shopping?" The woman propped her elbows on the table and fixed the old man with her sparkling eyes.

"In a manner of speaking. I was looking for inspiration, seeing what is popular this year."

"Do you have a lot of children to buy for then?"

"One might say that, lady, one might. And you? May I make so bold as to ask?"

The couple exchanged a look and the man took the woman's hand under the table.

"No. We don't have any children. Circumstances, you know…" his voice trailed off and she smiled sadly at him, shaking his clasped hand gently.

Over their mugs of cocoa, they chatted and the old man learned that they were planning to live together when the man could retire from his job in management. The old man agreed that he, too, wanted to retire, causing them to gasp in amazement that he was still working at his great age.

"Here, this is my house. It goes with the job. I want to give it all up and retire somewhere warm, somewhere to sit in the sun with an iced drink." On his cell phone he showed them a picture of the original Gingerbread Cottage, covered in snow, decorated with lights.

"Oh, how perfect," the woman whispered. "Snow and robins, polar bears, reindeer, sleigh bells, presents, laughter, spiced cookies… Sorry, I…" she wiped her eye. "I love Christmas."

"I think you do, lady. You have an air of the right kind of magic about you. And you, kind sir? Are you ready to retire if you found a more convenient post?"

The man nodded dumbly.

"This is my home." The woman offered her phone showing the small villa with a swimming pool. "It's in the south of France."

The old man's eyes held them both steadily.

"And you love children? You would like to exchange?"

"We're dreaming!" The woman's partner chuckled.

"No, sir. I came to look for a replacement. My wife and I are too old for this job. Congratulations, you have the position. Mr. and Mrs. Christmas. My very hearty good wishes to you both."

Dipping in his pocket he produced two red hats, which he handed over solemnly.

"Just one final thing. May I hear you both say, 'Ho ho ho! Merry Christmas,' please?"

ALEX BRIGHTSMITH
Picture Perfect

Maggie swept the hearth back carefully, suppressing a faint murmur of guilt. *They're only sparks burning in the soot*, she told herself. *If you leave them, they'll spread up the pot, and you'll have a chimney fire, and then where will you be?* But she failed to alarm herself. It felt wrong to sweep away the fire fairies on Christmas Eve.

She took out her ill-feeling on the fire, raking it out thoroughly before she made it up, then glanced at the clock, satisfied with her calculation. The coals would have burnt through to a welcoming glow by the time the photographer arrived, with just a flicker of flame, picture perfect, just as it should be. She roamed the room, moving cushions, tweaking the cards on the mantel to sit squarely, and then going back to set them carefully, artistically, askew again.

All the usual yearlong clutter had been swept away from the desk, replaced with five slips of colored tissue and a fine pen, and behind that an artificial scatter of acceptable litter—a slight indication of spilt glitter, a reel of festive tape, a few cards (though all their cards, of course, had been sent weeks ago) and even two or three spare stamps.

They annoyed her, the stamps. They must have been bought just for show, and they would have to be thrown away. There could be no parsimonious use of Christmas stamps in January for them, and Heaven forfend that they should be caught using this year's design next year. But there, that was the deal, and the secretary had done what was asked of him, and done it well.

She forced herself to go back to the window seat and tried to work. She had brought a report to review, one slim enough to slip into the drawer before she was interrupted.

It might be well known that she had a career of her own, but being a politician's wife, that career had better be invisible. Unfortunately, in selecting for brevity, she had chosen something dense enough to challenge her errant concentration, and she found herself watching the snow fall instead.

It amused her that, although even her husband's extremely efficient secretary could claim no credit for it, the scene outside was picture perfect too—the flurry just heavy enough to touch up the few faults in the view, hiding tracks and re-cloaking the wall where the boys had swept off the first covering for snowballs, but too light to cause any problems, even out here. No serious trouble on the roads, no interruption to the power, or to the phone lines, however much she might wish for it. And she did wish for it, suddenly, viciously, surprised by her own vehemence—one night with the man she had married.

A sudden crack from the fire startled her, but it was only the coals settling, sending a little flock of fairies—of sparks, she told herself firmly—up the flue. She picked up the report again, shrugging off her pique. Paul was a good man doing a good job, and the journalist's request had been a reasonable one, on the face of it, and by that measure difficult to turn down.

Sooner than she expected she found herself turning on the lamp. She checked her watch, irritated to have made so little progress, but found that she had only misjudged the overcast. She still had time in hand, and she read on placidly, soothed and reassured at last by the familiar hiss and crackle of the fire. When she finally heard the door, and excited voices from the hall, she slipped the report into the drawer, but she did not go to greet them; it was all part of the set scene. The perfect husband taking over the care of his perfect sons so that his perfect wife has a few hours to add perfect final touches to their Christmas. And never mind that the boys are, well, boys (demons as often as they are angels, and she would have it no other way) or that it takes a permanent staff of three to maintain this perfection, not to mention the hairdresser, the tailor, the tutors, and a dozen others.

It was only a moment before the door opened that she recognized the false note: there was only one adult voice in the hall, and it was unlike Paul to fail in drawing out his companion. Her sons had exploded into the room before it could worry her, and three boys, excited by a recent snowball battle, are enough to distract anyone from abstract concerns. She had risen to meet them without thought, and found herself swept into an embrace that would never have done for the cameras.

He laughed at her surprise, and joshed her for not noticing how much thicker the snow had been falling. It was lucky, he said, that the photographer had seen the forecast in time and called to cancel.

"So, how about those wishes?"

And he threw himself into the chair that had been only a stage set, and made it real, and the boys gathered eagerly around him, young enough to cling to the ritual even if they no longer believed in it. They had watched their wishes flare and vanish and be taken by the fairies before he realized that he had only one slip of tissue left.

He looked at her over their heads with that little boy lost look that was only for her.

"Have I been a bad boy? No wish for me?"

"No, darling, that one's for you. I had mine early."

LESLIE FULTON
THE CHRISTMAS LETTER

It was that time of year again. The annual Christmas letter extravaganza. The listing of accomplishments aimed to impress family, friends and neighbors scattered far and wide. Anna preferred the shock and awe approach. She liked to leave them gasping with respect and envy.

> *2013 has been a fabulous year for us. Lots of travel, of course, to Europe and Asia. Our best trip was probably Spain where Brian ran with the bulls in Pamplona. He looked so dashing dressed in white with that red kerchief around his neck. Brian managed to speed past them all, and was very thankful he wasn't gored. It certainly puts the spirit back into your life, he says and recommends that we all try it. Maybe next year for the kids and me!*

Anna pushed her chair away from the keyboard and sighed. "What a bunch of utter horseshit," she muttered to the dog, Peanut, an ancient terrier mix of indeterminate lineage. "That trip was a nightmare. Chris got sick and threw up the entire week, and Amy tuned out and listened to her iPod when she wasn't whining about missing her friends."

Anna picked up a pencil and chewed on the eraser, her brow furrowed in annoyance. She loathed writing Christmas letters, but Brian thought it was important and even made the trip to a special store to buy the cards. She hated the ones he chose. They always had gold foil inside the envelopes. The greasy slick taste of the glue made her stomach flip over.

Chris is playing soccer and continues to do well in his studies. He is having a stellar year and is thinking about his options for college. We're hoping he realizes his dream of becoming a doctor like his granddad or a lawyer like Brian. Chris is also singing in the church choir and enjoys socializing with his many friends after school.

"Doing God knows what. I think he's smoking dope." Anna nudged Peanut with her foot. He groaned in protest and halfheartedly snapped at her ankle. She noticed she had a hole in the toe of her sock. "I wonder if I should tell Brian about the porn magazines I found under Chris's mattress?" Her son befuddled her. What had happened to her cheery little guy with the missing baby teeth and the infectious laugh? Her sweet boy had turned into an incommunicative teen whose ringing cell phone seemed to be the only things that could animate his face.

Amy is our little angel. She is a perfectionist in everything she does and has made the cheerleading squad yet again. She is also teaching ballet to preschoolers and loves them to pieces. There's no doubt she's headed for great things!

Anna was worried about Amy. She couldn't remember the last time the girl ate a proper meal. When she did, it was junk and lots of it. Anna had found a green garbage bag full of vomit at the back of Amy's closet last week. She was drawn to it by the smell—that sickly sweet stench of rotting food and stomach acid. Amy spent most of her time in her room. She never came down for dinner anymore. Neither did Chris, for that matter. He was out with his friends. Not the ones from the neighborhood—but the new ones she didn't know from high school.

Brian didn't eat at home, either. He stayed in the city most evenings, working late. It was usually Anna all by herself, with Peanut for company, eating Campbell's Cream of Chicken Soup with a glass of Shiraz and the latest Martha Stewart magazine.

Of course, you all remember our dog, Peanut. Peanut is doing just fine and loves to chase balls in the park. He is ever the great companion, and I'll miss him when he's gone. He's fourteen now, and I dread the day he leaves our family for doggie heaven.

Actually, Anna couldn't wait. Peanut was a grouchy, incontinent little shit of a terrier-ist. The last time he paid attention to balls, much less retrieved one, was just before his got lopped off by the vet. Anna begrudgingly fed him his Purina Dog Chow twice a day only because she was afraid of the consequences if she didn't. Peanut was the type of dog who, if you popped off in his presence, would tear out your eyeballs and eat them with glee. You'd be found by the police with your entrails pulled halfway across the living room floor, the dog in the corner, panting and bloody. Anna hated Peanut.

And me? I'm just fine. Busy, busy, busy. I can't even begin to tell you all what I've been doing! Very happy—my family means everything to me—and I am so glad I can stay at home and take care of them. I consider myself blessed.

Anna snorted derisively. She took a sip from her teacup and looked at the clock above her computer, wondering if it was too early for a drink. It wasn't quite past eleven. In the morning. Anna loved her family, at least she used to. When Chris and Amy were young and needed her. When Brian used to come home at six, his arms full of flowers and groceries, his face alight and happy. Even the dog was tolerable back then. At least he didn't stain the carpet. Anna often wondered what would've happened if she'd kept her job in the city, at least part time. She had enjoyed working, making her own money, thinking for herself.

Wishing you much joy and happiness for the holiday season—from our house to yours during this so very wonderful time of Jesus's birth. We can't wait to hear what has been happening with you and your loved ones and look forward to receiving your letters.

Love always,
Anna, Brian, Chris, Amy and Peanut

Anna saved the document and sat back in her chair. She couldn't wait to get her first Christmas letter from old college friends and neighbors who had moved away. Oh, she had learned to read between the lines. It was a private language she'd mastered, unwillingly, many years ago. A lexicon that was only spoken—and understood—once a year.

SARAH NICHOLSON
The Angel Who Didn't Like Christmas

"Tinselitis?" Angel Anna raised an eyebrow suspiciously.

"I've got a sick note, signed by Dr. Laura. Had all the tests confirmed." His nose was already starting to twitch, must be that fake twinkling Christmas tree strategically placed to make Anna's desk look festive.

She tapped efficiently on her laptop. "Tin-sel-i-tis—an allergy to tinsel, glitter and sparkle. Such a shame this time of year," she said without a flicker of sympathy.

"So, if you'll just stamp this letter, verify that I'm too sick for duty I can be getting off home to recover." Jeff had it all planned out, a quiet Christmas in front of the TV for a change. He hated being an angel this time of year.

The telephone rang just as he sneezed.

Anna listened intently to the voice at the other end, nodding her head. Jeff found a handkerchief in his pocket and blew his nose with more force than necessary to make the point that he was still here, and he was sick.

"It seems the big man upstairs has a mission for you." Anna put down the phone while flashing Jeff her sunniest smile.

"I can't go down there at Christmas. You know how crazy those humans get."

"Special orders." She hit the send button on her laptop, and he was on his way.

It was angel rush-hour, thousands of them were gliding up and down the heavenly staircases off to work, each one chattering loudly, all decked out in their shiny best. Sequins twinkled in every direction like millions of eyes conspiratorially winking at him.

He shuddered, feeling hot and cold all at once. He should be in bed sleeping off this fever, but it was impossible to escape. Pushed along in the melee, he was trapped and descending toward earth.

Special orders. It was an honor, he supposed. He couldn't remember the last time he was singled out for an important mission, but before he had chance to ponder what it might be, he felt the ground give way beneath him.

"You have reached your destination." The voice was cheery yet mechanical as he gracefully floated to the ground.

He stood outside an inauspicious looking house, number 67 with a green door.

Most houses in the street were festooned in bright lights. There was a lopsided plastic reindeer opposite with a red nose that flashed rather alarmingly.

Jeff was glad this house was plain and ordinary looking. He shivered from the cold. There was snow on the ground, and he had no coat.

Unsure what else to do, he rang the doorbell.

It took an age before it was opened by an old man wearing a cardigan and slippers.

"If you're selling double glazing, I don't want it. Or a new driveway. I don't want a timeshare, and I've got enough tea towels to last a lifetime."

"I'm not selling anything."

"Well, you'll freeze to death out there, lad. Letting all my good heat out too. You best come in. Don't suppose you're a murderer? I'm too old for this life to care anyway and if you've come to rob me I've got nothing worth having."

Jeff followed the man as he shuffled down the hall into a stuffy overheated room with the TV turned up loud.

"I was just about to watch *The Great Escape*, you seen it?" He didn't wait for Jeff to answer, "Sit down then, lad. You're making the place look untidy."

The room was uncluttered with a TV, two armchairs, clock on the mantelpiece with a photo propped up beside it, mum, dad, three smiling children somewhere in a sunnier place.

"Family?" Jeff said, nodding in the direction of the photo.

"Son, daughter-in-law, in Australia. Now shush, film's about to start."

Sometimes it didn't matter where you went, heaven or earth, you were destined to be ordered about.

They watched in silence, each of them so caught up in the familiar story, there was no need to speak.

As Steve McQueen was shut in the cooler for the last time the man got to his feet. "Cup of tea?"

"I'd prefer a beer."

"Oh, what the heck. It is Christmas I suppose," said the man with a definite twinkle in his eye.

They chinked their glasses together.

"So, what's your story then? Turning up on an old man's doorstep on Christmas day out of the blue."

"Would it surprise you if I said I was an angel?"

"An angel! So what's your name then? Gabriel?"

"Jeff."

"That's not an angel name." The man shook his head, but he was beginning to grin.

"So, what's your name then?"

"Michael."

"Now, that is a good angel name."

"Pah! You can call me Wombat."

"Wombat?"

"Always fancied having a nickname. Don't you think it suits me?" He tried to twitch his whiskery face which made them both laugh. "It's good to laugh, ain't it? I ain't laughed properly for…well, for a long time."

Jeff studied the man, looked at the photo on the mantelpiece and surveyed a room devoid of Christmas cheer. He guessed his mission was just to keep this man company, not much of a special order but he had to admit this wasn't a bad way to spend Christmas.

They sat companionably, laughing at the festive entertainment on the flickering box in the corner.

All of a sudden, Jeff was aware of another presence; the room had become still and quiet for the first time. Anna stood beside Michael's chair.

"Is he gone?"

She nodded. "Peacefully and happy."

"And that was my special mission?"

She opened the folder she was carrying. "Last heartfelt prayer of an old soldier: *please don't let me spend my last Christmas on earth alone.*"

LISA SHAMBROOK
The Star Shone Brightly

Orion stretched languidly across the sky, winking at Danica or anyone else who might be admiring him, as he adjusted his sword and hitched his belt. Danica's eyes darted away as her luminosity flared in sudden embarrassment. She curled her lip, and her shimmer dulled as she slouched in melancholy.

Far below, the earth all green and blue, slowly spun, swathed in cotton-wool clouds, and Danica sighed. Twinkling stars, huge constellations of them, surrounded her but she felt invisible.

She didn't stretch across the night like Orion, was nobody's first point of reference like the North Star, and didn't hang glittering like the Southern Cross. She had no vast reach like the Great Bear and failed to shine like Sirius.

Danica's gleam dulled, and her sparkle was lost. The only thing that glistened was the tear that rolled down her cheek.

She didn't notice the kerfuffle that arose with the entrance of Virgo. She just moped behind Little Bear, until Little Bear whispered excitedly, "Virgo's looking for a new star…Spica and her sisters are exploring the Galaxy!"

"What for?" asked Danica, peering forward as glitter erupted in showers across the sky.

Little Bear shrugged. "They're not saying…"

Danica eased slowly out of her hiding place and strained her ears to listen.

"I'll go," boomed Orion. "I'm courageous, and I'll mark your place for you!"

"We're good!" chorused Castor and Pollux. "Two for the price of one!"

Below them Draco roared, "If you want a *real* star…"

Spica twirled, shimmering in her sapphire robes, and shook her head. "It won't work. You're all too recognizable. And Hercules, no, just no." She eyed the conceited constellation lounging almost out of sight. "It's just not going to happen! We don't need arrogance; we need humility, something new…"

Spica and her sisters sparkled and dazzled Danica as they swept across the blanket of indigo, dancing in and out of constellations, leaving a trail of glitter and restlessness in their wake. Danica stared after them, watching their effervescent cascade with eyes of envy.

The heavens stretched far and wide and the little star gazed as Virgo searched, hunting out the lesser known stars. She had no grand ideas and tucked herself back behind Little Bear, out of the way.

"I wonder what they're looking for then?" wondered Little Bear, "Something new, something new's happening. Look Danica, they're coming back this way…you should show yourself…"

"I can't," protested the little star. "I'm nothing."

Virgo swooped past Cassiopeia and as Spica swung by, she noticed Little Bear kick a little star from behind him. Spica turned her head, sprinkling sparks as she came to a stop, and the little star tumbled down toward her. Danica sprawled before the beauty, and her cheeks flushed again with hot, white light. She crawled backward whilst offering apologies, until Spica leaned down and smiled. "And who are you?" she asked.

Danica gulped, her iridescence dancing in an aura of pure light. "I'm no one," she whispered.

"No one?" Spica smiled softly. "You're not no one, you're the one we're looking for."

Little Bear grinned as his shy friend straightened her sparkling skirts and stared in wonder at the majestic constellation surrounding her. The sisters gathered Danica in their celestial arms and swept her off her feet. "You're the one," Spica whispered in her ear. "The one who can change the world. Now hurry away with us."

Several days later, a new star hung in the sky dressed in lustrous shimmering robes, only she wasn't a new star and she didn't have any new clothes. Danica sparkled and scintillated, lighting a dark, inky sky, and three wise travelers used instruments to plot and follow her glowing trail. Whilst they journeyed, she shone with effulgence and guided both angels and shepherds, and glistened with everything she had, as a newborn cry rose from the stable heralding change in the world below.

And all around, stars twinkled and gleamed, but none shone as brightly and as joyfully as she.

MICHAEL WOMBAT
Claustrophobia

Oh bum. How the jingle bells did this happen? Bloody centuries I've been doing this; how come all of a sudden I get stuck? I mean, yeah, in this dark I can see the sum total of sod all, but that's never stopped me before, even in really tight squeezes. The old Santa Wriggle usually gets me through any gap, as well as pleasing the elves at the Boxing Day Hullabaloo. Heh, it's all in the hips, you know.

It's become quite the dance at the party—great lines of elves and fairies, not to mention the missus, all doing the old Santa Wriggle. OK, yes, I call our celebration the Boxing Day Hullabaloo, and that's a British thing and I'm originally Dutch, but I just like that name, you know? Boxing Day—the day after Christmas according to the Brits. It trips off the tongue, don't you think? The Boxing Day Hullabaloo. Mind you, that won't be happening this year if I can't move myself.

The old Santa Wriggle is not doing it; not this sodding time. I can't shift, neither up nor down. I blame the missus' new mince pie recipe; the one with extra butter. I ate fifty yesterday. Might have gained a few inches, I suppose.

Bloody hell, it's pitch-black, my nose is pressed against filthy rotting bricks, I've got soot up my nose and I do *not* like it. I feel pressed in, squished tight. I might never get out, and then what? No more toys for good little girls and boys, no more coal for the naughty sods. It'll be a bloody disaster.

What's that, you say? Santa shouldn't swear? Piss off; you'd be letting out a nonstop stream of all the swears you know if you had to go through what I do once a year. Up and down all those sodding chimneys, and all within twenty-four hours? It's not bloody easy! Yes, yes, my time-slowing ability thingy helps, and that teleportation device that Elf Ansafety came up with proved invaluable when people started living in places without chimneys. But you know, that's not the whole job, not by a long chalk.

Have you ever thought what happens when a reindeer decides to have a poo right up there on someone's roof? Of course you haven't, your minds are all full of tinsel and glitter at Christmas. Well let me tell you, you can't just leave it up there, it'd stink for days. And imagine the questions once it was found. Nope, Muggins here has to shovel it all up and put it in the poo sack. Think yourselves lucky I don't get *that* mixed up with the sack of toys. Ah well, at least the reindeer don't drop their *"doings"* in flight, cause that'd be a terrible Christmas present for anyone down below.

This isn't getting me shifted, is it? I feel all closed in, trapped, and I'm sure there's not enough air in here. And what the hell's that sharp thing sticking into my bloody arse? Come on, Nick, see if you can reach round to have a feel. Ah, loose brick. Maybe if I can wiggle it out... *Ouch!* No no, bad idea, bad idea. Better leave it. No one wants a sharp brick corner poking them up *there*. I'd better see if I can call that lazy cow of a fairy down here, see if she has any bright ideas. Maybe she can magic me free.

OI! NUFF, WHERE ARE YOU? GET DOWN HERE!

Bet she's sitting on Dasher's antlers having a right old gossip. What's the use of having a fairy PA if all she does is sit about swapping recipes and talking about soap operas with reindeer?

I bet my beard's as black as, well, soot by now. I probably look more like Brian Blessed than Sinterklaas. You don't know Brian? Give him a Google, then you'll know what I'm on about. Mind you, Brian wouldn't be up a chimney, would he? Probably down at the pub having a pint of ale, like a man with sense. Unlike me, with no sense, stuck up a chimney and probably never going to get out and I might stop breathing soon and oh no oh no…

NUFF, GET DOWN THIS CHIMNEY NOW OR I'LL STICK YOU ON THE TIPPY-TOP OF MY TREE NEXT YEAR!

Calm down, Nicky, calm down. Panic will do you no good at all. Maybe if I twist my arm like this—whoa, at least that dislodged something. I think I can get my fingers to it, I…*ew!* It's all bony and feathery and, *ew*, gooey. I think it's…*ugh*, dead bird, probably, and I poked my fingers into it. Ick ick ick.

NUFF! WHAT THE HELL ARE YOU PLAYING AT UP THERE? BRING YOUR WAND DOWN HERE THIS INSTANT, YOUNG FAIRY!

Bumholes, got a mouthful of grit there. Tastes like burnt—wait, what was that? I'm sure I heard something. Yes, there it is again. Noises beneath my boots. Sort of a scraping and a tapping. Is someone down there?

"Yes, ma'am, it is early! Never mind, I'll soon have the fire roaring and then the children can come down!"

Uh-oh.

All the Christmassy Things
A Poem by
LaDonna Cole

I do love all the Christmassy things;
twinkling lights, reds, blues, and greens.
Wishing for snowflakes to land on my tongue,
sleigh rides, snow angels. O what fun!
Rudolf and Frosty, and even the Grinch,
are the tales of which the season is drenched.
Streets come alive with elaborate lights,
arches of holly and mistletoed heights.

Pageants of toddling Marys and Joes,
and rubber baby Jesus swung by his toes.
Precious blonde angels with crafted wings,
drip glittery sparkles as they boisterously sing.
While shepherds and wise men with sniffling noses
wave to their kin and strike silly poses.
Proud parents armed with photo apparatuses
are eager to update their Facebook statuses.

Bing and Karen sing our favorite renditions
of Christmas carols, our finest traditions.
Potlucks and parties will top off the year,
spreading around the best Christmas cheer,
With white elephant rounds of ten-dollar treasures,
give to co-workers giggles of pleasure.
Elf on the shelf over here and there,
sneaks into action as Christmas draws near.

Cocoa steam curls into the air
as we snuggle together and Christmas tree stare.
Fireplaces stay busy with warm delight,
and display our stockings arranged just right.
The scents are spiced with cinnamon and apple.
Our appetites with restraint do grapple.
Stuffed greeting cards are becoming rare,
as digital media is easier to share.
But how I adore opening the mail to find
gorgeous pictures and greetings and hails.

Mostly I love the traditions cast,
as I watch my children repeating the past.
Like stealing the babe from his prominent place to hide
'til he's born on holiest of days.
Or calling my family on Christmas Eve Day.
"Christmas Eve Gift!" I'll be first to say.
Then laugh with delight to hear them reply,
they'd said it first, much faster than I.
Then later that night we'll bundle up tight.
We'll worship together beneath candlelight.

We'll lift our voices in carol with choir,
extoling the savior, Earth's peace our desire.
Arm in arm to Mimi's we'll roam to
kindle the fires of hearth and home.
We'll stay up late sharing stories and song,
then plead with the kids, "Bed is where you belong."
Finally we'll surely see Santa's red light
wending his sleigh to us through the night.
Cookies on mantel, kids rush to their beds
too excited to sleep, they'll cover their heads.

But oh when they wake on bright Christmas morn'
a mountain of presents has taken fine form.
Beneath the tree all crisp and bright,
bow-topped presents will meet their sight.
"Who will play Santa?" they call over mugs
in Christmas jammies all warm and smug.
As presents divide into small piles,
with name tags to match the thankful smiles,
We'll take turns opening, one at a time.
I'll pay close attention when they open mine.

The best gift to me is the rapturous glow
on my family's faces o'er the gift I bestow.
Then we'll gather the wrappings with hugs all around,
thank yous, and tears, amidst grateful sounds.
Moms start cooking the fabulous feast.
Dads clear the mess, then prop up their feet
To watch a game and mastermind
the assembling of toys or batteries to find.
The ruckus of games, motors, and gifts,
everyone glad, saturated in bliss.

Don't get me wrong. All isn't sublime.
There'll be one who steps out of line.
But once again we'll let go and forgive,
find ways to love, to live and let live.
Families and yuletides are a wonderful mess,
but for each one I feel simply blessed.
For this season is worth all that it brings.
That's why I love all the Christmassy things.

Other Anthologies
by bhc press

Available at booksellers everywhere
in softcover & ebook*

*most titles available in hardcover & audio

CPSIA information can be obtained
at www.ICGtesting.com
Printed in the USA
LVOW11s0948281117
PP12920800001B/1/P